Black Mountain

Carol Chandler

Black Mountain

Excerpts of this novella have previously appeared
in *Four W*, *Idiom 23* and *Offset*.

Black Mountain
ISBN 978 1 76041 365 1
Copyright © Carol Chandler 2017
Cover photo: dark forest fog © andreiuc88
Author photo: Brigitte Grant Photography

First published 2017 by
GINNINDERRA PRESS
PO Box 3461 Port Adelaide 5015
www.ginninderrapress.com.au

The nightmares came less often now, an owl beyond the branches, light shining fiercely through the trees, the darkness of their trunks densely packed together, my brother Liam's body consumed by flames.

A house with thin spires was visible in the distance, the moon reflected in the window of the bus, as I left the siding and walked towards the car park.

I could see Freya near the bridge, long-limbed and ghostly. Her hair trailed down to her waist, pale as shimmers of ice, her small face giving her a look of innocence and expectation. The blouse she was wearing seemed familiar, a soft fabric like silk, a pattern of aqua blooms. The bodice was crimped around the sleeves and the material hugged her figure in a flattering way, the sleeves hanging low under her arms and exposing the pallor of her skin.

I walked up to her quickly, noticing a large dog by her side. Freya kissed me and I glanced at the dog uneasily. We began walking towards the bridge.

'Tyler's back at the house,' she said. 'He's looking forward to seeing you.'

I was conscious of an unspoken language between us. The dog was walking by Freya's side and I glanced down at it again. It had a predatory appearance, a pointed muzzle and slanted eyes.

When we reached the car, Freya helped me put my backpack in the boot, the dog darting around her legs. 'It's Tyler's dog,' she said, noticing my gaze and smiling at it. 'His name is Jet.'

I remembered that Tyler had another dog years ago which I'd been afraid of.

We climbed into the car and Freya glanced across at me, the glow of headlights illuminating shadows around her face. There were lines near her eyes that had appeared in the intervening years since their baby Scarlett's death, a tired look.

'How's Tyler going?' I asked, conscious of my hesitation.

'He's OK,' she said. 'He wasn't responsible for what happened, you know. He was completely exonerated. It was a cot death.'

She started the car and began driving across the bridge, the dog shifting constantly in the back seat, growling a little, as if it sensed my fear.

'I'm really glad it was sorted out in the end,' I said. 'I thought you were going to leave with all the confusion and stress.'

'I thought about leaving, but Zac's still here, so Tyler wanted to stay.'

Zac was Tyler's son from a previous relationship. He'd had him when he was only seventeen, so at twenty, Zac was only six years younger than me.

The dog was still moving in the back seat and I began to feel increasingly unsettled as I gazed out the window at a wide sweep of sky, burning mists shrouding the plateau and rolling in from the coast across forests, a light flashing amongst the clouds.

'It's so beautiful here,' I said. 'I'd forgotten how beautiful it really is.'

'Yes, that's another reason we decided to stay. People didn't understand Tyler's way of thinking, at first. Now they accept him. He's a visionary.'

I could barely contain myself when Freya described Tyler as a visionary. It was true he was a talented craftsman, the handmade wooden furniture he'd created and the house he'd built, turrets and arches, windows like a church. They'd sold it when they needed money for Scarlett's medical problems.

The forest began to thin and I remembered following a clear path through the darkness towards an uninhabited house.

Up ahead, I could see wide streets and a roadhouse, a small strip of dilapidated units where Freya had lived when I first came down here.

We turned off the highway and began travelling towards the west, both of us silent.

'I guess this place was really too small for you,' said Freya, at last. 'I don't blame you for leaving.'

'It was a difficult decision. The teaching job came up and I felt I couldn't knock it back.'

Freya said nothing as I stared out the window. It was a while ago now but I wondered if she resented my decision.

'It's quite a way from town,' I said, changing the subject. 'Are you lonely out here?'

'No, not really. We came here to escape all the gossip, although we have neighbours now. They're not very nice people, so we may move again.'

This was the first time she'd explicitly mentioned the town's reaction to what had happened, the suspicions about Tyler, that he'd somehow been instrumental in Scarlett's death. I had a feeling that she was resigned to it.

Freya turned down a track, heading south through trees and bush. She drove slowly so as not to damage the car on the rocks that were strewn along the road and, as we rumbled further along in the darkness, I noticed a wooden house and small garden of shrubs up ahead. The dog had stopped moving and was quiet now. Perhaps he was used to me.

We left the car and walked through the front gate. There was an old swing in the front yard of the house. It was partly obscured by a hedge from a ramshackle place next door. As we walked along the path, I noticed berries had fallen to the ground from a tree. Passing through the entrance, I saw a bay window with panes of glass angled away from each other, a large crack where something had hit the glass. Freya had said someone came by several weeks ago and threw something at the house.

We followed the corridor, past a living room with a dark box seat near the window. The heavy material of curtains was visible against the glass and Freya walked inside and quickly closed them. We were in the middle of nowhere, so I gathered she felt oppressed by the neighbours.

When we reached the end of the corridor, she led me into a small room. As she turned the light on, I put my bag down and walked over to look outside. It was dark in the yard, but the shapes of trees were swaying in the wind. A light was on in the house next door, and through the hedge I could see the figure of a man moving back and forth along the fence.

When I turned, Freya had an ironic expression on her face.

'Let me know if you have any problems with him. He's a nuisance, thinks he's better than everybody else.' She opened the door to an old wooden cupboard. 'You can put your clothes in here and there's a chest near the door.'

I began unpacking my clothes, hanging them in the cupboard and folding them into the chest. Freya sat down on the bed. She had a serious expression on her face and I walked over and sat down beside her.

'I'm so sorry about Liam,' she said.

'I'm having nightmares about it,' I replied. 'I'm not really sure what happened, whether it was an accident or arson.'

Freya's features were controlled and tight and I realised I'd hit a raw nerve.

'You'll find it gets better with time,' she said gloomily. 'I've heard people say they forget their loved one has passed away and automatically want to talk to them about something they think would interest them. When I see a child the age Scarlett would be now, I find myself thinking about her all the time.'

Feeling distressed, I touched her hand gently. I knew what she meant. I'd been saying the same thing myself. If I'd said too much about Scarlett, though, it would have sounded false or inadequate, particularly as I didn't have a child myself. It might have been even worse if I'd had one, because it would have been a child that had survived.

She stood up and returned to the window. 'We hadn't seen Liam for a while,' she said. 'He shut people out. Nobody really knew what was happening.'

I went back to unpacking my clothes and when I glanced up, she was still staring out into the darkness. The silken material of her blouse outlined her figure, billowing gently near her arms. I finished unpacking and we left the room together, walking down the corridor to the kitchen.

Tyler was leaning up against a bench when we walked inside. He looked very much the same, in spite of everything they'd been through, the same olive skin, wide feline eyes, broad nose and full lips.

I walked up to him and kissed him on the cheek and he responded a little awkwardly, as if he hadn't been expecting it.

Stepping back towards the bench, he smiled at me distantly. 'How's your teaching going, Sarah?' he asked, as the dog lifted its head, craning towards him.

Zac, Tyler's son, had been a bright child who didn't fit in at school. He'd been involved in a car accident before I'd left. Karin, the woman who had been driving, had been killed. Tyler was still leaning up against the bench. He shifted his leg slightly, still gazing back at me. Freya had told me he was concerned about the way things were going with Zac. He began to fidget and I noticed the tension in his body, remembering how he was quickly bored by conversations. He was wearing a workman's singlet, short shorts and sandals that showed off his muscular body. He'd always worked outdoors and was constrained within a four-walled environment. Tonight, though, he seemed edgier. Zac had been living near a group of people further out in the mountains and Tyler didn't like them. There was one man in particular he couldn't stand, a psychologist whom he referred to as a religious nutter.

'I've been enjoying teaching,' I said, wondering if Tyler would rise to the bait. 'Do you remember the last time I came down here to visit you? You were living in the mountains.'

'Yes, I remember,' Freya replied.

The day of the visit, the waterfalls had frozen into icicles. The lake outside the house had frozen too, ancient trees and tree stumps with wire disappearing quickly into ice and mud. I'd climbed to the top of the hill, leaving Freya and Tyler at a playground with ropes. The view had been magnificent; an alpine field with a lake, mountains in the distance. Cold had numbed my face, an absolute stillness cloaking the hills.

'It was real red-neck territory,' I said. 'Particularly where Connor lived, with gunshot holes in the road signs.'

I'd always wondered why Freya and Tyler insisted on staying there. Freya had said they liked the remote aspect of the area. The surrounding hills were gouged out of the landscape, surreal, a sickly mustard colour. It was difficult to tell whether the environment was the result of mining, or the more natural sculpture of glaciers but the colour and lack of vegetation gave the place an unearthly feel.

'Are you going to see Connor while you're here?' Freya asked, interrupting my thoughts. 'We haven't seen him for a while.'

'I'm not sure. He's not the same person I was in love with. I miss that person, but I suppose he doesn't exist any more.'

'I guess none of us is the same,' said Freya. 'I always felt that Connor never did anything he didn't want to do, even though much of what he did was good. After you broke up, he said you had issues. I said to him, "Who doesn't have issues?" and he looked shocked.'

'I can just imagine Connor saying that about me.'

I could see a faint smile on Tyler's face as he walked outside, where he began playing with Jet in the yard.

I watched Freya draining some pasta that Tyler had been cooking on the stove.

'Don't take too much notice of Tyler's moodiness,' she said. 'Apart from Zac, he's on edge because they're talking of laying off staff at the park.'

Tyler was throwing a ball for Jet to fetch outside in the yard. He did it in an agitated way, as if he were releasing tension, throwing it aggressively. I remembered my first meeting with him years ago, his defensive nature. He'd been rifling through a packet of photos, endless pictures of a nondescript patio with dark plants. I'd found myself struggling to think of something to say, until we arrived at photos of a house with a stained wall that looked like water damage. I'd glanced at Freya for some kind of clue but she'd seemed entranced, with an indulgent look on her face, as if she were a proud mother humouring a gifted child. At the same time, though, she seemed to look up to Tyler because he was older and had a brash type of confidence.

'I'm planning to go to Black Mountain, tomorrow,' said Freya.

I frowned at her, remembering how steep it was. 'Why do you want to go there?'

'I haven't been for a while. Do you want to come?'

'I don't know. It's so steep.'

Tyler walked back inside with Jet. I could see the irritation in his eyes and I glanced away at a wooden horse on the dresser. Freya had broken it as a child and Alison, her foster-mother, had glued it back together with dark plasticine. It was a stallion and the carving was so detailed, you could see the veins and sinews, like the anatomy pictures in old textbooks.

A light flicked on from the back porch in the house next door.

'I don't think you should go to Black Mountain,' said Tyler, glancing out the window towards the light. 'It's too much for you.'

Freya began serving up pasta from the pot. 'No, I'll be all right. Is Zac coming this weekend?'

'No, I don't think so,' Tyler replied.

He seemed preoccupied and I sensed he wanted to talk to Freya alone.

It was late, and after dinner I said goodnight and left for bed. When I reached the bedroom, I looked to see if the porch light next door was still on but it was dark outside.

Climbing into bed, I drifted off to sleep, the soft warmth of the pillow pressing against my cheek as I sank down into the nest of blankets and sheets.

In the early hours of the morning, I awoke, drifting between dreaming and waking. Hauling myself up out of bed, I walked to the window. The light was back on next door and a man was in the yard, walking towards the bush I watched him disappear beyond the trees as I listened to the noises of animals outside. Jet began to bark and I climbed back into bed.

I drifted off to sleep, my dreams broken by Jet's barking, until light began to stream into the room. Leaning forward in the bed, I noticed the cold cut-glass crystal of a perfume bottle, the facets of the glass intricate and shiny in the light. I pulled myself up out of bed and walked to the window. Jet was in the yard and I became distracted for a moment, when I noticed someone further out in the bush beyond the trees. When I looked down again, Jet was beneath me on the path. He looked up at me and I flinched, unnerved by his eyes, dark, with a hint of amber and the menacing appearance of his jaw, sharp teeth and strong bone structure, like a wolf. Instinctively, I moved away from him.

When I glanced up again, there were two people in the neighbours' yard: a man with bulging arms like a boxer, his head square with narrow features, and, beyond him, near the house was a woman. She had a vulnerable look. Her head nodded forward and even from a distance, her skin looked cracked and worn, sagging. There was the sound of a door opening, the shuffling of footsteps, and a young man came to join them, slightly built, almost adolescent, with short hair and the light fuzz of a beard. The older man turned towards the fence, his face creased and weathered, clothing dusty and crumpled. Standing back a little near the curtain, I watched him turn towards the house.

I got dressed and left the room, walking down the corridor to the kitchen. Freya was swishing fruit around in a large bowl.

'I saw your neighbours in the yard.'

She carried the bowl to the table. 'For years there was no one living there. Jet's original owner is a friend of theirs. Liam was friendly with their niece, Lola. She left town and they haven't heard from her. I think they blamed him because he was encouraging her to leave.'

'Maybe I should talk to them, about the fire. They might know something about it.'

Freya sat down and began trailing her spoon amongst the fruit.

'You'll get nothing out of them, Sarah. They're very unpleasant people to deal with.'

Through the glass doors, I could see Jet near the tree, running back and forth. Tyler was standing between the branches, one foot wedged between the trunk and a branch. He appeared to be pulling off a loose branch as Jet walked towards the back porch, his large head misshapen, out of proportion to his body.

'Jet isn't a great-looking dog, is he?' I said, without thinking. 'He reminds me of Tyler's other dog, Moon.'

'We like him,' Freya replied, looking offended. 'Beauty's in the eye of the beholder. He's a good dog really, and he had a horrible time with a friend of his previous owner. The guy's been in jail for assault.'

I noticed Freya was wearing shorts and her belly was slightly swollen against the tight fabric. She caught me staring at her.

'Are you?'

'Yes, I'm pregnant.'

'Freya, that's wonderful. I'm really happy for you.'

'I was going to tell you, but with the miscarriage I had, along with Scarlett, I didn't want to say anything. I've only told a few close friends.'

I walked over and hugged her. After Connor and I had been together for a while, I'd wanted to have a baby but he hadn't wanted the responsibility. At least he was honest about it, I guess.

Tyler had climbed out of the tree and was walking towards the neighbours' yard. I wondered how he felt about the pregnancy. He'd been ambivalent about having Scarlett and had told Freya when they were first together that he didn't want any more children. Zac was enough, he'd said. He had too many problems with him. Freya was ambivalent about it herself, but then something changed and she convinced Tyler that having a child together was the right thing to do. I remembered the miscarriage.

'I know you said you wanted to go to Black Mountain but maybe you shouldn't go.'

'No, it's all right. I know my own body.'

I looked at her in a concerned way and she glanced away from me.

There was a piece of driftwood in the corner and an ebony cane, black and tipped with silver, a face painted on the handle, one of those stylised 1920s faces, like a kewpie doll.

'Tyler found the cane in a second-hand shop,' Freya said. 'His taste can be a bit eccentric sometimes.'

The driftwood had a darkness about it and was hollowed out and sculptured with sharp wedges, the delicate fissures and crevices in the wood like the spaces between the rocks on the coast. I'd seen Tyler shaving off pieces of wood from the smooth surface of driftwood. He used to whittle away at it, waiting to see what form took shape. Whatever emerged was added to his collection of sculptures, the curious assortment that he kept at the back of his shed. Sometimes he carved from stone; simple faces, long and medieval, their solemn eyes like the cat's eyes stone from the Emporium where I'd worked with Tyler's friend Nathan, in town.

Jet began barking wildly and when I glanced outside, Tyler was running towards the house.

'Those bastards,' he said, his voice shaking with anger.

He ran inside with Jet and I noticed blood on the dog's side. Freya grabbed a cloth and began staunching the blood.

'You should've heard them,' Tyler said, sounding distressed. 'I went over to see if they'd seen him. 'Don't fuckin' accuse me, mate, if your dog wanders around.'

'Jet might have scratched himself on Zac's wood.'

'No, I don't think so,' said Tyler, his voice still shaking.

Freya began dabbing some antiseptic on the wound. 'Just leave it Tyler. Don't provoke them.'

I began to feel nervous, sensing that Tyler was up to something.

'Is it OK for Jet to come with us to Black Mountain?' Freya asked, glancing up at him.

'Yes, of course,' said Tyler, impatiently. He bent down and helped Freya put a dressing on the wound.

I went and gathered my things and when I returned Tyler and Freya were waiting for me.

Tyler's moodiness increased as we left the house and climbed into the car. He was brooding about something and I presumed it had to do with either the neighbours or Zac. Freya and I began talking about the time we'd walked the entire length of the beach, but I sensed Freya was preoccupied as well, as there was a false pleasantry to the way she was speaking.

There were very few cars on the highway and I began thinking about the night Scarlett died. I'd visited the pub with Connor and had tripped on the way, falling to the ground in the darkness. I'd felt the rough surface of the ground beneath my hands and when I glanced up, there was a large poster of a boy on the wall, pale skin, eyes wide and knowing, slightly averted as if looking down at the viewer. His body was bare-chested and slim, ribs outlined against ghostly flesh. Underneath the photo, there was a mobile number.

As we drove along the highway, I stared out the window at fields with scattered trees, isolated farmhouses in the distance.

'Hopefully it won't rain,' Tyler said, glancing up at the sky.

We drove for some time until Tyler pulled over near an area of scrub. Jet seemed more settled now but I had an odd feeling of disconnection as we climbed out of the car and began walking along a path that led down to the ocean. The track traversed an area of spinifex and as we reached a verge, I could see the sand stretching out ahead of us to the headland, dunes rising to the left, tufted with grass. Grains of sand blew onto my face, hitting my cheek, dark clouds scurrying across the sky.

Freya and Tyler began walking ahead of me along the shoreline. I walked down to the water's edge, gazing out to sea when I noticed Freya run down to the waves. She began wading in the water, skirting the waves. I walked back towards the dunes and sat down on the sand where Tyler was sitting with Jet. He appeared to be staring at a point in the distance, beyond where Freya was wading.

There was no way I was going into the cold water but I became conscious of a subtle warmth from the sun which was now shining through the clouds, so I took off my jumper and leant back.

Tyler was still staring out at the sea as Freya returned from the surf. She had abandoned the shorts she had on earlier and was wearing jeans which were wet around the hem. She pulled a jumper out from her bag. It was a tight fit when she put it on, but her body was still slender, strongly built, almost Amazonian, her long blonde hair shiny in the light. For some reason, I remembered how both of them had been ambivalent about having Scarlett, but I tried not to think about that, conscious that things were different now, that the coroner had definitely decided it was a cot death and that they no doubt wanted this baby they'd both conceived.

Tyler stood up and began walking towards the bush. He was striding briskly ahead and Freya and I had difficulty keeping up with him. Freya quickened her pace and caught up and they pulled ahead of me again. It was difficult to hear what they were saying, possibly something about the neighbours, as I heard the words 'next door' and 'Darcy'.

The path became steeper and we began climbing along a ridge towards the mountain. They were still ahead of me but when I caught up they were talking about the time Freya had stayed up north with Alison, her foster-mother. It had been a difficult time for them as it was directly after Scarlett had died.

'Maybe we should move back there to be closer to Alison,' Freya said. 'It might be better with everything that's happening.'

I wasn't certain what she was talking about, whether it was something to do with the pregnancy or Zac.

The bush began to thin, and we emerged onto a cliff, the sea stretching immediately below us, glistening in the sunlight, extending out towards the horizon. The view was magnificent and I glanced at Freya, who appeared deep in thought, with a troubled expression on her face. She'd told me they'd scattered Scarlett's ashes in the sea, but I was certain it was further north. My legs began to shake as I stood on a rock very close to the cliff.

Tyler turned away and began climbing further towards the summit. I tried to ease myself off the rock but my legs froze completely and I began to panic. Breathing deeply, I managed to move a little, but then my legs began to wobble. If they wobbled any further, I would slip and go over the edge. The trembling became more violent and I sensed someone behind me. When I glanced around, Freya had disappeared and Jet was in the bushes. I could see the sharpness of his teeth, white against his dark fur. He was watching me intently and I looked anxiously for signs of aggression. To my alarm, it appeared as if he was about to pounce. If he leapt forward, he would knock me off the edge, but he didn't move, just sat there staring at me. I tried speaking to him softly, but he began snarling a little.

Waves of panic gripped me and I tried to ease myself further off the rock, but my legs were still frozen. They began to tremble violently again and I took a few deep breaths as Jet began to growl. Tyler emerged from the bush and Jet rushed to his side.

When I turned further, I noticed a mocking expression on Tyler's face and my heart began beating quickly. 'Where's Freya?' I asked, breathing deeply.

Jet began to bark more wildly and Tyler grabbed him by the collar but his hand became caught.

'Damn dog,' he said. He yanked the dog violently which increased my sense of panic. Then he disentangled himself. 'Give me your hand,' he said.

I could see that he was checking himself, suppressing his emotions, so I gripped his hand, but I tried not to focus on his expression, which was stern and angry. He carefully helped me ease my way off the rock as I heard rustling behind me.

After a few seconds, Freya appeared through the bushes. There was a look of anxiety on her face when she noticed Tyler's expression.

'Sarah couldn't get down,' Tyler said.

I worked my way further down the path, grasping onto his hand, but he was holding it so tightly now, I felt uncomfortable.

'I don't know what happened,' I said.

'Have you ever been afraid of heights before?'

'No, not really.'

We began retracing our steps back to the car and Tyler pulled ahead. I felt more relaxed now that he was further ahead and I glanced at Freya who was silent. As I caught up to Tyler, I glanced across at him. He seemed more at ease and I remembered Freya telling me once that his father had been an army man who regarded all frailty as a sign of weakness.

'I think our original plan to move to the mountains is better,' said Freya, as we reached the beach. 'Get away from the neighbours. We can also keep an eye on Zac.'

'I don't know,' Tyler replied. 'I think the neighbours are going to move.' He said it ominously as Jet began snapping at a bird near the dunes. 'Damn dog,' said Tyler. 'I don't know why I took him on.'

He ran ahead and brought Jet to heel as we began following the path back to the road. Freya was lagging a little behind as Tyler pulled ahead. Once we'd reached the car, Jet leapt into the back seat and I felt uneasy as I climbed in beside him.

The sun was shining faintly through the clouds as we began driving back.

Freya and Tyler began talking about the mountains again.

'I think it's a good idea,' said Freya. 'The house is in a good position and we need to keep an eye on Zac. I don't want to stay where we are any more.'

Tyler nodded grimly, staring ahead at the road.

The mountain range was in the distance, a mist descending like a phantom on dark peaks, and I noticed a large sandstone house, with attic windows, set back from the road.

Tyler turned off the highway and continued on along the dirt road towards the house. There were several cars parked outside the neighbours' house as we pulled up.

Jet leapt out of the car when Tyler opened the door and when we walked inside, the bean bag was in a different position. There was an intense smell of something cooking, like grilled cheese and pickled onions, someone playing a guitar next door, the repetition of chords.

'Zac's been here,' said Tyler, surveying the scene. 'As usual, he didn't tell us he was coming.' He sounded irritated.

I walked down to my room as Freya disappeared into her bedroom. Pulling another jumper out from the cupboard, I noticed the yard next door was empty. Jet was in the bushes near the fence, nosing around a plant. There was a man on the neighbours' porch. He had his back to me and only the silhouette of his body was visible, long-limbed and thin, the upper half of his torso muscular. I heard him whistle and Jet looked up before turning back to the fence, craning his head towards the path. He appeared to be listening or watching something. The fence was broken between the two houses so Jet must have wandered across.

I stood there for a moment, studying him, but I couldn't see anything further beyond the fence. The man moved away towards the end of the house. He still had his back to me and I could only make out the wiry outline of his body, dark hair and clothing. His shoulders were broad and he was wearing boots with a low heel worn down at the side. Turning the corner, he disappeared down the side passage and I waited for a moment to see if he reappeared. The porch remained empty and I wondered if he was the man I'd seen disappearing into the bush the previous night.

Leaving the window, I returned to the living room, where Freya was sitting on the couch. She was wearing a tangerine shirt and the sheerness of the material made her pregnancy more obvious.

'I saw someone walking off into the bush last night,' I said, thinking about the way Jet had been standing near the beginning of the path, leaning forward, as if he could see someone further out beyond the trees.

Freya looked up at me. Her face was composed but with a hint of tension, her pale hair brushed back in a loose ponytail.

'He was tall, thin, like the man I just saw on the porch.'

'It might be Radic,' she said, 'Lola's father, the girl Liam was friendly with, the one who left town. Radic thinks something's happened to her, although there were sightings of her up the coast.'

She picked up some knitting and began unravelling the wool onto her lap. I watched her wrap a strand of wool around one of the needles, pulling it tightly and inserting it into the loop with a careful precision, manoeuvring the needles back and forth in a way that put me on edge. She was now concentrating on her knitting, no doubt thinking about the baby.

An intense sadness took hold as I thought about Scarlett, the way she'd been found in her crib, and an image of her came into my mind. I imagined her lying there, cold and inert but lovingly wrapped in blankets by Freya.

'You won't run into Radic,' Freya said, glancing up at me. 'He lives further out beyond the gully. I can understand how he feels. Liam shouldn't have gotten involved with her.' She stopped her knitting and was looking at a newspaper on the couch.

'What do you mean "gotten involved with her"? How old is she, anyway?'

Freya pursed her lips as she counted the stitches. 'Only seventeen.'

I watched her rearrange the wool and studied the intent way she was focused on the needles, a slight crease on her forehead.

'Maybe he wasn't involved with her,' she said, still studying the wool. 'But Radic's convinced there was more to it. They like a fight that family. Good haters.'

I walked over to the window, bothered by what she'd said. We were on the other side of the house next to an old shed surrounded by bush. There was another shed further back near the garage. Freya was concentrating on her knitting and I walked out to the porch, to see if I could get a better look at the yard next door.

Jet was outside, near the fence separating the two houses, and I moved closer to see if I could see the neighbours' porch. It was set back further, near my bedroom, but if you looked back from the window you could see it. An odd silence, something palpable and heavy, seemed to emanate from the neighbours' house and I studied it for a moment, before turning and noticing the path that led off into the trees towards a gully. Connor had mentioned something about Lola to me on the phone, but he didn't think there was anything to it. Liam hadn't seemed all that worried, he'd said.

I left the steps and walked towards the path, thinking about Freya, how tired she seemed. Jet walked up and began nuzzling my leg and I flinched from him, remembering my experience on Black Mountain, the way he'd watched me on the edge of the cliff as if he were about to pounce. Tyler's other dog, Moon, had been a similar breed. He'd dragged himself back from the highway after the car accident that killed Karin, the woman whose car Zac had been a passenger in. Moon's leg had been bloodied and matted but he had borne the pain stoically. There had been a dumb acceptance that Tyler as master would do something about it, but at the same time, no expectation whatsoever, just a fatalistic immersion in the pain. It had been impossible to save him and Tyler had been distressed by his death. At the time, he said he'd never own another dog, so I was surprised he'd taken on Jet.

Jet remained nearby, before wandering away towards the house, shuffling up the steps and disappearing inside. I stood there for a moment, before leaving the garden and walking along the path that led into the bush, still thinking about Tyler and Moon.

The path was bordered by ferns, a series of plants constructed in rings up ahead, an elevated rock like a pulpit. I wondered why Freya had gone back to Tyler after their separation following Scarlett's death. It had seemed a good time to end the relationship, as there was friction between them, arguments about who was to blame for it happening. But then Freya had taken a defensive position when the community began to turn on him, insisting that he was a good man. 'I know myself what it's like to be judged,' she'd said. 'Or constantly misunderstood.'

Down below, I noticed the sheer drop of a gorge. A shimmering haze of mist shrouded the treetops, the scent of rotting leaves, resinous and earthy, strewn along the ground, reminding me of the autumn leaves of childhood. The grotto must be something that Freya had planted, I realised, as I glanced up at the canopy of leaves above.

Trees towered above me as I continued on along the path. Down below, I could see a river in a ravine. Steadying myself, I clambered down the slope to the bank, careful not to slip on the twigs and leaves. The surface of the water was a dark brackish colour like tannin. A long tree trunk had fallen, and lay partially submerged across the water, tree ferns near the bank, their branches spreading like umbrellas, beside a dense thicket of undergrowth. The log had a moss-covered sheen, and I had a sense of existing deep within something, cocooned within a comforting darkness, amongst ferns, trees and water.

There was a rustling noise and when I turned, Jet was in the bushes. I stared back at him, surprised that he'd followed me along the path. He stood there watching me silently and I smiled at him uneasily. I turned away and he began following me. He appeared to be deliberately trailing me, following and watching.

As I reached a rock jutting outwards into the river, I saw someone walking in the opposite direction, a man wearing a similar flat-top hat to the one I'd seen through the fence next door. He was younger than the other man, with dusky olive skin, his hair unruly and long. He looked like the man I'd seen on the porch, but I couldn't be sure.

There was a surly expression on his face and as he approached, I noticed a long dent in his skin from the inner corner of his eye across his cheek which detracted from the regular appearance of his features. There was also an odd sheen on his skin, like sweat, as if he'd been running or working hard. He drew up close to me and I stepped back a little, noticing a scowling expression on his face.

'Taking the dog for a walk, are you?' he asked sarcastically.

His hat was tipped towards his eyes, which were dark, almost black, with a quick glimmer of intelligence or cunning. I watched him purse his lips, and to my alarm, I noticed a gun by his side.

'Tell them to keep their fucking dog away.'

He delivered the words in a threatening tone and it was then that I noticed a small dog with tan fur cowering in the bushes. The man jolted his head around when he saw me looking beyond him. He whistled to the dog and it ran up to him, standing meekly and obediently by his side.

Jet began barking furiously and the man stared back at him. I watched his hand move towards his gun.

'Call your fucking dog off,' he said.

The man glared down at Jet again and I had a sense that he was used to bending both people and animals to his will. He looked at me curiously and I saw a flicker of recognition in his eyes as he studied me for a moment, compressing his lips grimly, before turning away and whistling to his dog. I watched him move away from me, sauntering down the path, until he disappeared beyond the trees towards the river.

My heart beat quickly as I studied the way he walked, a rhythmic gait, almost like an experienced tracker. He looked similar to the man I'd seen striding into the bushes the previous night and perhaps on the porch as well.

When I glanced around, Jet had disappeared. I called out to him and eventually he appeared, looking distressed. He stared back at me for a moment, as if I'd failed him in some way, and appeared to be waiting for me to make the first move. His body looked tense, ready to react as he had on Black Mountain, and my heart began racing again.

I steadied myself and glanced back along the path to see if I could see the man. He'd already disappeared completely beyond the trees and when I looked back at Jet, he was a little to my right, standing apart. He appeared to be keeping to himself, and I watched him pause for a moment, nosing around a bush. I remembered Moon again. Moon was smaller and used to bark continuously, running back and forth across the yard. He always leapt at you eagerly, wagging his tail furiously. In some ways, Jet actually seemed more reserved, more wary. Then I remembered how he'd been mistreated by a friend of his previous owner.

Jet began following behind me again. He made me feel nervous, the way he avoided walking by my side. Oddly enough, the man's dog had appeared well cared for, unlike Jet, who although loved by Freya and Tyler, looked damaged and mangy, like a cur.

There was a lake in the distance, surrounded by forest and outcrops of moss-covered rocks. The water was darker towards the centre, a brilliant light shining through the branches that leant out across the lake.

I thought I heard footsteps behind me and when I turned, Jet had disappeared. The bush was silent now and I continued walking, my feet squelching through puddles of mud, as I disappeared off into a mental stillness that was punctuated by the intermittent sounds of the forest, the cries of black cockatoos and the rustle of leaves in the trees.

As I climbed higher, the bush began to thin and I found myself in a clearing surrounded by a ring of trees. Jet had disappeared completely now and I wondered angrily why he had abandoned me.

Down in the valley below, past kilometres of uninhabited forest, a river wound its way towards the coast. In the distance, a tiny cluster of houses was visible amongst the fields.

The tension dissipated from my body, but the feeling of safety was an illusion. Nothing could be seen beyond the treeline, only the valley directly in front of me below. I stood there for a moment, anxious, conscious of my solitary state, not knowing what was beyond the trees, aware only of the outward appearance of the bush.

Again, I had no choice but to continue back down through the same impenetrable thicket of wood and foliage. As I walked on, my confidence grew, and as the bush began to thin and I reached the highway, the tension vanished once again from my body.

I breathed in deeply and looked around me. The road was silent and as I continued towards town, the scent of roses drifted into my mind, a bottle of rose perfume which I'd pulled out of my desk before I'd come down to visit Freya and Tyler. Connor had given it to me long ago and I'd kept it.

As I turned a corner, I began to feel uneasy again, with that odd sense that I had on the beach, of being confronted by someone or something out in the open, that feeling of connection and disconnection. The highway stretched ahead of me, an endless strip of black, bordered by bush that encroached onto the perimeter of the road.

I continued walking until I could see shops near the outskirts of town, the Emporium in the distance. There was no one on the main street but as I approached the Emporium, I noticed a man standing in the doorway, smoking a cigarette; thin, dressed in jeans and boots, long, straggly hair draped around his shoulders. He made room for me as I passed by, stepping back a little, but not nearly enough for me to get by easily. Another man stood at the back of the shop when I walked inside. His hair was close-cropped, and he had a goatee beard, and a muscular body covered in tattoos. The man at the door followed me in and walked over to the one at the back.

I moved away a little, looking through to the back room, to see if Nathan, the owner, was there.

'I was inside for eighteen years,' I heard one of the men say. 'You know who I'm talking about. She's the one who put me away.'

I turned around and the man with the tattoos walked up and stood immediately in front of me. He stared directly into my eyes with a bemused expression and I flinched, unable to control my reaction.

'Hey, do you think I look good?' he said. 'I've been inside for eighteen years and haven't been with a woman in all that time.'

His features were strongly defined, while his complexion was that of a very young man. There were no marks or lines on his face at all, which seemed odd for someone who'd been in jail for eighteen years.

'You'll do all right.' I said, trying to keep my tone as bland as possible.

An expression of almost childish relief flickered across his face, as if he'd been found acceptable to a woman in the outside world. 'Are you married?'

'Yes,' I lied.

'It doesn't matter.'

'It matters to me,'

There was an unnerving silence as we continued staring at one another for a moment.

Then suddenly his smile broadened. 'I was married once, myself.'

I waited for him to continue but he made no other comment. His voice was a little faint with a slightly unpleasant tone and neither of us said anything further. I glanced back at his friend, who was also silent, and I wondered what had happened to his wife, whether she'd abandoned him during his years in prison, or whether he had, in fact, killed her. Then I remembered his comment, 'She's the one who put me away.'

Neither of us said anything, then at last he turned and gestured towards his friend.

'I was at a party last night and an unsavoury thief stole the diamond stud from my ear.'

I frowned as I remembered my father telling me once that thieves were low in the jail hierarchy. He'd been convicted for my mother's manslaughter and apart from Liam's funeral, I hadn't seen him now for some time.

Moving away from the men, I walked through to the back room, where there was a mound of paperwork on the desk, a fridge and small sink with a kettle and cups. There was no one around so I walked into the yard, where I found Nathan tinkering with a bicycle near a shed.

'Sarah!' he exclaimed. He stood up and hugged me. Then he pulled back a little as if he were conscious I was in a fragile state.

I felt the familiar grief rising in my chest and a sensation of compression in my throat as I thought of Liam. Choking back tears, I could see Nathan smiling at me sympathetically. He looked away, embarrassed by my shaken state, and squatted down to the bike, giving me time to recover.

I breathed in deeply, feeling as if something had become trapped in my throat, a sensation of suffocation. As I gazed down at the bike, I remembered the police description of the fire in which Liam had died, that disturbing image which always came to me at night of his body burning. It induced a sickening sensation of nausea and terror. I tried to suppress it now as I stared at the shiny reflections in the spokes of the wheel and the blackened grease on Nathan's hands. The thickness of the grease distracted me as I thought of the charred remains of Liam's house and the darkened image of his body in the flames.

'You're staying with Freya and Tyler, aren't you?' Nathan asked, completely unaware of my disturbance.

I watched the spokes turning as he pushed the wheel back and forth, the light on the silvery surface of the metal. It distracted me for a moment, as I thought of Liam's bike, the dark leather of his boots and the uneven stones on the surface of the road.

'There's a girl who left town,' I said. 'Liam told me he was friendly with her. She's the niece of Freya and Tyler's neighbours.'

'Oh, that,' he said. 'She's a friend of Zac's, too. I heard she was sighted in town, further along the coast. Didn't they tell you that?'

I looked away from him towards the shed at the back of the yard and when I glanced back he was watching me closely.

'Liam kept to himself. Didn't talk much. He was good with Freya and Tyler, though.'

There was an accusatory tone in his voice and I realised he was insinuating that Liam had stuck by Freya and Tyler while I was the one who had abandoned them.

I glanced over at the shed as Nathan picked up the wrench and twisted something on the wheel.

'Tyler's always had a lot of friends,' he said. 'I'm surprised more of them didn't stick by him after the baby died.'

'I thought they were mostly Freya's friends. Freya's always seemed to be the dominant one because she's a talker.'

He put the wrench down. 'That's deliberate. It's to build Freya up, give her confidence. She was so anxious about becoming a mother.'

At first I thought this was ridiculous but then I thought back to the times when I'd noticed that Tyler was unusually quiet when Freya was talking. On a couple of occasions, he'd looked very contained, almost like a parent listening to his child, pleased at her progress.

A young man walked into the yard, thin and gangly with sandy hair, his T-shirt emblazoned with the name of a heavy metal band. 'Where's the basketball?' he asked, loping up to Nathan.

Nathan nodded towards the garage and waited until the boy had left the yard. 'Freya recently contacted her birth mother. Did you know that?'

I wondered if this was another dig at my not knowing what was happening, and not being around to give them support.

'She mentioned it to me on the phone. She didn't really want to talk about it. She doesn't talk much about her past, Tyler either. I know it's a sensitive issue, the fact that Alison fostered her.'

Nathan smiled conspiratorially and I began to feel uncomfortable that he might have been drawn into the gossip network.

'The contact went badly,' he said. He looked tense but there was a knowing tone in his voice as he put the wrench down again. 'She seems to have shut down. No one can get anything out of her. Perhaps you can. You were close to her once. It's a shame she had a falling out with Alison.'

'What happened?'

He raised his hands helplessly. 'You know how it is with them. It's complicated. Alison hates Tyler. Poor Tyler.'

I wondered why he was so sympathetic to Tyler when, like everyone else, he'd been suspicious of him after Scarlett's death.

'I don't know that much about it,' he said. 'Something happened when Freya was young. You know how she was depressed after Scarlett was born. I think it brought back memories.'

I stared back at him, irritated by his insinuating tone. 'A lot of women have postnatal depression and she recovered from it.'

'I suppose so, but she had to deal with the baby's death. Don't you think she behaved strangely? She was distant. She can be like that, a bit cold, don't you think? Connor thinks Tyler idealises her.'

It was true Freya had been distant but then some women react like that out of shock.

'Freya was upset too.'

'Maybe, but there were a lot of problems after Scarlett died. Remember how she and Tyler separated? I think this is only a temporary reconciliation. Tyler's distracted by Zac of course. But it's difficult for him having to deal with Freya as well. She's high maintenance. I heard from Jim McCulloch. He had a short relationship with her, when she and Tyler separated. It didn't work out. Alison says she's difficult too.'

I knew Freya could be difficult and that she'd been depressed. Who wouldn't be after losing a baby? She'd also told me she was having therapy and that Tyler had been going with her. She referred to it as 'family therapy' but after speaking with her on the phone I had a sense that she'd moved on to other issues and Tyler was still going with her. I'd thought it ridiculous that Tyler was accompanying her to the sessions. They seemed to have developed a real co-dependency relationship, something previously so unlike Freya. She looked up to Tyler but she was never dependent on him. Now, I wondered if there was something more complicated that she needed support with.

'But what if Freya gets over it and Tyler decides to move on? What happens to Freya?'

'Oh, it's no problem. They each have a half-share in the house.'

His tone was measured and I wondered if there was something to what he said. It was just like Nathan to be thinking of the financial implications. Or was it more likely that he was avoiding the emotional ones because it might mean there was more to their relationship than he wanted to admit? I stared at him suspiciously, remembering that at one point he'd been interested in Freya. That was how it was down here, people waiting for other people's marriages to fall apart so they could move in on them in a predatory fashion, taking the place of the recently divorced or abandoned partner. Also, if Freya and Alison had had a falling out, who knew what Alison was saying. I began to feel uncomfortable again, thinking that he'd misinterpreted things.

'Who are those men in the shop?'

He looked at me, baffled.

'Ex-cons. One of them said he'd been in jail for eighteen years. Are they friends of the Lonegans, that family in the mountains who were dealing ice? Wasn't Zac friendly with the son?'

Nathan propped the bike up. 'I don't know about ice. Tom Lonegan was just dealing a bit of weed.' He changed the subject and began talking about Bob and Vonnie, who lived in the mountains, how Zac had seen them recently and how they'd been over to Greece and missed the warmer weather. 'You should talk to Zac. He always liked you.'

Nathan looked uncomfortable now as if he'd said too much and I followed him through into the Emporium. The men were no longer there and I noticed a boy with blond curly hair, thin pointed face and dark eyes, standing near a rack of postcards. He was dressed in a black overcoat and he pulled a card from a holder, before moving over to a stand with jewellery and key rings.

'You might be right about Freya,' Nathan said, glancing at the boy. 'Maybe I've misinterpreted things. Her circle's widened. They've been talking about moving to the mountains, a lot of interesting people out there now. That psychologist guy, Matt – she's been doing a bit of gardening for him and Zac uses his place as a studio. He's done some artwork. Some of it's not bad. He can draw well, animals and landscape, that sort of thing. He's not really into people.'

I walked towards the door with him, conscious that he was insinuating something again when he'd mentioned the psychologist and Freya, something in his tone. I had a feeling that he disliked him as much as Tyler did.

We said goodbye and I left the shop.

The last time I'd seen Freya, there'd been an awkwardness between us which had bothered me, a definite stiffness as we'd said goodbye. She'd said something about me being her conscience and I'd felt a sudden surge of loneliness, as if separated from the common tide. She'd left me at the bus stop and there'd been a sense of inevitability as if I'd already known there would be no one there. I'd waited, suspended in the emptiness, conscious that during that moment, Freya would be getting back into the car and driving off towards town. There was a feeling of release and I'd had no great desire to run after her, or try and find her. Instead, I'd waited, somehow hoping the bus would appear. Freya's distance had troubled me at the time, as if she were hardening herself, becoming more guarded and detached.

A ute pulled up outside the newsagency and a man wearing a lumberjacket climbed out onto the footpath. He was solidly built with a heavy beard and leant forward towards someone whose face was concealed inside the car.

I walked past them towards the newsagency, looking back as I walked inside. A middle-aged woman with a worn and wasted look stood at the counter, bent over what looked to be a spreadsheet. She was wearing a cheap cotton blouse with a cherry print and I moved past her to a stack of newspapers nestled behind shelves of cards. The woman gave me a cursory look, the television blaring in the background.

I returned to the counter with a newspaper, conscious that someone had walked past me into the shop. The woman glanced up and I shifted my position, craning forward. Squinting for a moment, she smiled at me with the air of someone eager to know something, while pretending detachment for form's sake.

'You're Freya's friend, aren't you? Sarah, isn't it?'

She leant forward on the counter, clearly irritated that I was looking at what was going on behind her. I could see that she wanted to say something about Liam's death but was wrestling with the fact that she didn't know me well. I stepped back and reached into my pocket for the money.

'I saw Freya the other day,' she said, taking the money and ringing it up in the till. 'She mentioned they're moving to the mountains.'

I could see a man standing near a filing cabinet inside the room. He had heavy boots like the ex-cons in the Emporium, with a design like a curl at the end. When I glanced back, the woman was frowning at me.

She had an open face, with fine hair clustered around her forehead in soft grey curls, pale blue-grey eyes, limpid like the sky.

I smiled back at her and began folding the newspaper under my arm. 'Yes, they are moving but I'm not sure when they're going.'

She frowned at me when she saw I wasn't going to say anything further and I watched the man disappear around the doorway.

I left the shop, pulling my jumper tighter round my body as a sudden gust of wind rattled an awning. I tried to spread the fabric down to my hands so that they were covered like mittens. One of my fingers became caught in a part of the sleeve that had worn through and I pulled it out quickly, so that the sleeve didn't unravel. An image of Freya and her knitting came into my mind, the way she'd concentrated on winding the wool around the needle, inserting it in the loop. I'd always envied Freya her concentration, but she seemed unusually focused now as if nothing else mattered. Everything had been filtered down to the finest point. The wind whipped against my back as it whistled through town, and I walked quickly towards the bus stop.

Looking back along the road at the highway, I noticed the way it disappeared as a dark strip in the distance around a sharp bend. The car I'd seen earlier pulled away, driving through town, and I watched it vanish.

Liam had said very little about Lola to me. He'd only mentioned that he was helping a friend, although he did say he was wary of Freya and Tyler's neighbours, 'Stupid people,' he'd said. 'But cunning.'

Glancing along the street towards the highway again, I studied the way the bush encroached onto the road, the dense tangle of trees and scrub. The bus turned a corner in the distance and began crawling along the road towards me. It pulled up nearby with a chugging sound and I climbed on board, remembering the man in the forest, the anger in his voice and the way he'd stared at me. There had been a real hatred in his tone as if he were bitter or blamed Freya and Tyler for something. He seemed to see Jet as their emissary. I remembered that very brief look of recognition too, and wondered if he was thinking of

Liam. Liam and I had similar features, pale olive skin, high cheekbones and dark curly hair. Our eyebrows were strongly defined and people often commented that they looked like black parentheses above our eyes. The way the man had looked at me was unnerving, an intense stare, like the chill wind that I was now feeling through a crack in the window. There was something discomforting too about the way he'd stood directly in front of me. It reminded me of the man in the Emporium. He'd done the same thing, standing immediately in front of me while staring directly into my eyes.

The bus arrived at the turn-off and I climbed out onto the highway and began walking along the dirt road towards the house. The cars I'd seen earlier had gone but as I walked towards the gate, I had a sense that I was being watched, as if there was someone inside the neighbours' place, a visitor, or a person who didn't belong there. I noticed the swing in the yard, rusty and slightly skewed, beneath the trees. Zac used to play on the swing as a child, and I remembered him silently watching the movement of trees in the breeze.

Freya had given me a key the night before and I unlocked the door and walked inside. There was a room to my right with a wooden bookcase and leather-bound books, a case on an old chest of drawers, containing what looked to be scientific instruments. The instruments were delicate and appeared to belong to a bygone era, something a scientist or craftsman might use. One of them was a long silver hook which had a slightly menacing air. Another had a silver circle like a mirror. There were also several instruments that looked like surgical knives. I studied them carefully, picking them up and running my fingers over the cold metal surface, examining the shiny glint of silver.

I remembered Tyler's friend Billy, who lived out in the mountains, how he used to skin animals, and I tried to banish the image from my mind of Tyler and Billy killing wallabies and deer, my grandfather butchering animals in his shed.

Some of the leather-bound volumes were medical textbooks. I pulled one off the shelf and, flicking through, I recoiled at photographs of diseased bodies, faces and genitalia blurred to protect the dignity and privacy of the subjects. As I flipped through the pages, I was confronted with graphic photographs of people afflicted by illness. The photographs were black and white, from another era, and the people didn't appear real. It was almost like seeing a hidden part of one's grandparents that one had never seen, something personal and private, images from the past.

I put the book back on the shelf and walked over to the desk, trying to think why Freya and Tyler might have books like these. It was an expensive leather desk and the chair was heavy, the kind you would see in a lawyer's office. The whole room had the impression of coming from the past and I tried to recall if Tyler had inherited any of this from his family, but I couldn't remember him saying this. All I knew about his father was that he had been in the military. Tyler had never mentioned his mother, so I knew nothing about her. She was a shadowy figure who seemed to feature little in his life.

Sinking back into the chair, I studied the covers of the books, gold writing down the spines. There was a stack of files on the desk. I glanced at them quickly, articles about real estate, legal documents and the park where Tyler worked, then I pulled myself up and left the room.

No one was in the kitchen when I walked inside. Through the window, the darkness of Jet's coat caught my eye. It was a sooty grey, like volcanic dust, something from the bowels of the earth, and it struck me again how he reminded me of a wolf with his dark slanted eyes, pointed muzzle and ferocious teeth. Tyler was walking towards him. He looked angry and was striding in a similar way to the man I'd seen in the bush, loping but purposeful. Jet followed him and they left the garden together, heading off into the trees, birds circling, as they disappeared off towards the gully, down and down.

*

I'd always had a sense that there was something repressed or coiled within Tyler, waiting to unleash itself when you least expected. It was obvious he'd known since childhood that he didn't fit in and once I'd told him he had an anger management problem. He'd laughed at me and said I needed to do something about my own ferocious temper. Studying the bush where Tyler and Jet had disappeared, I knew that I'd been avoiding things that had affected Liam and myself, different elements of our personalities and the past.

I sensed a movement to my right and when I turned, Freya was squatting near the fence, in a vegetable garden. She'd said very little about the time when she and Tyler had met. It was when she lived further away along the coast, near the town where Tyler had worked.

Freya was close to an apple tree, digging in the earth, amongst silver beet and pumpkins laid out in rows. There was a beautiful symmetry to the way they'd been planted, which was so typical of Freya, the colours and the textures of the leaves. Freya used to bottle jam and fruit, preserving them for winter, plump apricots swimming in syrup and rich tomato relish, delicious on toast. It had seemed idyllic in those days, the house they were living in with its leadlight windows and elaborate wind chime that tinkled in the living room; a willow tree with a tree house in the yard, amongst the fallen leaves on the lawn.

Studying the bracken and tree ferns, I glanced back to the left and noticed someone on the porch: the young boy I'd seen in the morning with the older man and woman in the yard. I recognised the slightness of his build and the clothing he was wearing, baggy jeans and shirt that was too big for him. He stared back at me for a moment before moving to the end of the veranda as if determined to get away. I moved closer to the window but once again only his back was visible as he pressed up against the railing in the corner. He paused for a moment, tapping his foot, then he disappeared around the side of the house.

A flame flickered in the grate of a heater, warming the room, a rich aroma of sauce scenting the air, something that Freya had been cooking on the stove.

The table was made of dark heavy wood, while the chairs had curved backs and conical seats with bands of colour. The floors and walls were also wooden; square panes of glass in the windows, heavy beams in the ceiling. Glancing up, I noticed earthenware pots on a shelf. Beams of wood ran diagonally across the wall, and the floors were limewashed, a wooden rocker in the corner.

The room was like a museum, everything coordinated and carefully placed, almost obsessively. This was Freya's doing, I realised. She liked creating order out of chaos, something idealised or different to what was around her, what she'd been brought up with. It was different too to the minimalist chaos of my own flat; the reverse, in fact.

When I glanced to my right, Freya was standing in the garden. She followed the path towards the house, her expression defiant as she walked into the kitchen. Her eyes had a guarded or hunted look, the expression that came onto her face when she was wary or hurt. I wondered if she and Tyler had been arguing and that was why I'd seen him heading off into the bush with Jet.

I didn't know whether to broach the subject of her birth mother, but decided to go ahead because she'd mentioned it on the phone. I had a sense before I came down that she wanted to confide something.

'I went for a long walk,' I said, as she placed some herbs down on the table, thyme, rosemary and marjoram. I could smell their cleansing scent. 'Nathan was at the Emporium. We had a long chat and he mentioned something about your birth mother.'

'Don't take too much notice of Nathan. He likes to gossip. You know he used to be interested in me.'

I noticed the intense blue of her eyes, like the centre of a flame. Her hair was pulled back from her face and there was a tear in her shirt near the waist which I hadn't seen before.

Freya sat down at the table. She appeared to be contemplating the stem of a piece of thyme and I waited for her to speak. I studied the full curve of her lips, which were set in a stubborn line, and the length of her hands, which were pale, although a little roughened from working in the garden.

Picking off pieces of the thyme, she began pushing them around the table, forming a pattern of circles. She glanced up at me, frowning a little, and I decided she must be angry at Nathan, not me, the fact that he'd divulged personal information in a gossipy way.

'You said you met up with your birth mother a long time ago but then you lost contact completely.'

Freya looked away towards the window. 'Darcy, my birth mother, was meeting me out of obligation.' She picked up the thyme again and began fiddling with the remaining leaves. It was obvious she'd been expecting this all along, felt rejected and was hitting out.

'Did she say anything about your birth father?'

'No. She didn't want to go into the past.'

I wondered if the situation was as harsh as she made out. Freya could exaggerate sometimes. I watched her form complex circles with the remaining leaves of the thyme, concentric rings like crop circles.

'I hardly remember my birth father,' she said, glancing up at me. 'He left when I was young. Darcy wanted to clear her conscience or was afraid I'd try and contact her. She knew I'd managed to track her down through other people. It was obvious she'd made a life for herself which had nothing to do with me.' She picked up fragments of the leaves, compressing them slowly between her fingers.

'She should be proud of you. And you're expecting her grandchild.'

'Well, she's not.'

Her voice was icy and, upset by her reaction, I tried to think of something wise to say. 'If she was distant, it might be because she learnt to cope like that and it was her way of having to block off emotions from the hurt of the past and giving you up.'

Freya stiffened as if this was difficult to take. 'Sarah, I know you like to rake over your own past. It used to upset Liam all the time.'

My heart beat quickly as I studied her, wondering what Liam had said to her. Freya's expression was distant now and I sensed her agitation. Her eyes had a curious hue, like the deep blue of the sky as it transitions towards night, that period at dusk when animals reclaim the darkness, owls, possums and gliders, sheltering in the shadows of the trees.

I watched her playing with the herbs and remembered a snake slithering into the house, coiled in the corner of the room, a bowl of oranges on the table, the rich vibrancy of the fruit and the sheen on the snake's skin, slick and leathery as it slithered away towards the porch.

She brushed some of the leaves back and forth along the surface of the table, frowning slightly. I wondered if she was similar to her biological mother. Nathan was right: Freya could be cold herself sometimes. She often kept you at arm's length as a self-protective mechanism. It upset me, too, that she'd compared me to Liam, implying that he was in some way more resolved when nothing could be further from the truth. He'd been just as disturbed by our father's domestic violence and our mother's death as I was. I watched her closely for a moment and her expression shifted slightly. She smiled at me more warmly now and appeared to be waiting for me to speak, but I said nothing as she looked away again.

Knowing I was being deliberately provocative, I said, 'So she said nothing about your birth father?'

'No. He left, that's all I remember.'

Her abruptness was almost comical and I hesitated before saying anything further. I watched her gather the remaining herbs, pushing some of the stray leaves off the table with a wide sweep of her hand.

'Perhaps you should see her again. Give it another go.'

'She did talk about coming down here. I don't know if I want that... I mean, with the baby.' Her voice faded as she stood up from the chair.

She looked uncomfortable now, as if she didn't want to go into it and I felt guilty that I'd pushed her. There was clearly something about her family that she didn't want to discuss and perhaps it was best left alone.

'Darcy's had a number of relationships,' she said. 'Maybe it's just as well I don't remember. She lives further north up the coast and I haven't seen her for some time.'

There was something unconvincing in her tone and I glanced around at the ordered kitchen, the earthenware pots on a shelf on the wall, and the neatly coordinated furniture. Freya probably felt even more compelled to create order in her life after her unsuccessful meeting with Darcy and her difficulties with Alison. She'd always had an excessive need to clean when stressed and I watched her move over to the sink and begin washing up. It was the opposite to my chaotic approach, how I let things go to block off anxieties and stress.

'How's Alison?' I asked, testing the waters.

She hesitated for a moment, before putting a plate in the rack. 'She and Tyler haven't been getting on.'

She had her back to me and I could see the tension in her arms, the jerky movements.

I remembered the books and instruments in the study. 'There were some interesting things on the shelves in the front room. Where do they come from?'

Freya turned to face me and I watched the awkward way she leant back against the bench, tipping slightly.

'Tyler's grandfather gave them to him. He kept them because they're like anatomy books. They help him with his sculptures.'

'Is that why he kept the instruments too?' I was unable to keep the sarcasm from my voice.

'Yes, that's right, Sarah. Some of them are good for fine detail. You read too much into things.' She turned away and pulled a jar out from the cupboard, fiddling with the lid.

'I'm going to see Connor,' I said, observing how irritated she appeared. 'He might know more about what was going on with Liam. I mean, this business with the car following him and the fire. Liam told me someone was following him a week before he died. I have nightmares about the fire at the cottage. I feel I should have been there to protect him. It was really only shortly before his death that we got back in touch.'

'I don't know about Connor. We haven't seen him for a while. He was going out with a Polish woman but they've broken up. He seems to like exotic women. I guess that's why he was attracted to you.'

She said it ironically and I remembered showing Connor a photo of my maternal grandparents, who I'd been closer to than my parents. My grandfather had been in the Italian partisans in World War II and I'd been very proud of him. It was something to make up for with my parents. In the photo, my grandparents were in an interesting pose because their bodies were at an angle, looking almost directly into one another's eyes; neither looking up, nor down. They were smiling and completely at ease with an expression of love, respect and friendship. Tyler was there when I'd shown Connor the photo and he'd studied it closely.

He'd taken it from me, holding it carefully in his hands. 'They look like they love each other,' he'd said. 'You can see it in their smiles. My parents weren't like that. They always argued, hated each other.'

He'd gazed back at me, as if he wanted to say something but couldn't. At the time, I'd thought we had more in common than I'd realised.

I glanced down at the flecks of herbs on the table now as Freya pulled some cups out from the cupboard. When I glanced up, I noticed my reflection in the window, shadowy and distorted. Shocked by my weariness, I wondered how I was going to manage during the weeks ahead as I tried to find out what had happened with Liam.

Freya was near the sink. 'Did Connor tell you he was going to go into business with us? Him and Greg, his friend in town.'

'Was it some kind of import business, or something about the marina?'

'An import business. We need to do something because Tyler won't be getting much work at the park. I've been talking to Matt about it.'

I remembered Nathan's comments about Freya and the psychologist. 'Is Matt the psychologist in the mountains, the one that Tyler doesn't like?'

She moved over to a green vase with a base shaped like a twisted vine. 'Yes, the one in town was too expensive and it was pointless, really. I talk to Matt. He's a friend. I don't see him professionally. Tyler was friendly with him at first, then he went off him.'

Glancing up, I noticed numerous jars of condiments in the cupboard behind her. They stretched back to the interior of the shelf, foreign writing, the outlines of a language I didn't recognise, a jar with a picture of a woman, the curving shape of her body dressed in billowing pants.

Tyler's old boots, caked with mud, were in a small room to my left. Close by, there was a rusted shovel. There were several rows of plates in the cupboard, too many for Freya and Tyler alone. I wondered if they were left over from the time they'd had large parties when they'd lived in the mountains, or if other people had been staying here. People used to come from the coast, others from as far away as the city.

I picked up a stem of thyme, inhaling the scent of the remaining leaves, before pulling them off piece by piece towards the end. There was a book nearby about mountain climbing and I pulled it over, flipping through the pages. Tyler was fascinated by the obsessive drive of mountain climbers, the uneasy balance between friendship and the solitary competition of the climbers. We'd watched a documentary once about a team of mountaineers who'd made it to the top of a peak. Several of the climbers had died on the descent and another had fallen into a crevasse. Somehow the man had hauled himself out, crawling back, little by little, until he'd finally made it back to base camp. Tyler had been mesmerised by it, whereas I'd found it distressing. The bodies of the other climbers were left strewn at the point of death, irretrievable and frozen forever in the icy waste. People were either drawn to look at them or avert their eyes in their relentless pursuit of the summit. We'd argued about extreme sports, whether it was really worth it, and Tyler had become quite heated about it.

I glanced at Tyler's boots again, positioned near a sink in the laundry, not far from a gardening implement, a long prong-shaped fork that was probably used for shifting the soil. There was a shovel nearby with clods of earth. It looked heavy, something that would be difficult for Freya to use. She'd taken to gardening with a vengeance after Scarlett had died, constantly out amongst the plants, keeping to herself, wanting to be left alone. There was a sack pushed up against the wall, jeans, heavily soiled. They looked like Tyler's and I wondered what he'd been doing. Nearby there was a piece of wood. It reminded me of the sculptures Tyler used to do on their property, smooth and featureless, their faces elongated, arms, narrow and claw-like.

I stood up and stretched my arms, feeling the tension in my muscles relax, thinking about the strangeness of Tyler's sculptures. I noticed the vase on the table again. It had a twisted curve near the rim and was heavily patterned with a leaf design, ornate, the complete opposite to Tyler's sculptures, which were minimalist or generic.

Leaving the room, I walked down to my bedroom, passing by the living room, where the curtains had been pulled across. This seemed to be the default position in the house, keeping the curtains closed to shut out the neighbours.

Inside my bedroom, a grey matted cobweb hung like strands of thread in the corner. I reached up and touched them, wondering why Freya hadn't cleaned them away. This seemed unlike her and I brushed the threads away lightly with my hand. They stuck to my fingers and I peeled them off, piece by piece, trying to flick them away.

The murmur of voices drifted across from the yard, hushed words, jovial and friendly, interspersed with laughter. There was a man standing behind the fence, obscured by the branches of a bush. He had a grizzled and shadowy growth visible on his cheeks. His boots could be seen through a gap, resting on something like a can. Only the upper part of his torso was visible, bulky with a denim jacket, some kind of transfer, a circle with a red border.

I shifted my position near the window. The heavy bulk of the man's body was partly obscured by the palings. I noticed a broken pane of glass above and remembered the broken glass out the front of the house. You could probably throw something quite forcefully and break it if you tried. Perhaps the neighbours had thrown an object vindictively, just to annoy Freya and Tyler. People could be petty like that around here. I reached out and touched the crack, feeling the surface against my fingers, raised and sharp, like the ridges of the perfume bottle on the dresser.

I shifted my position to the right, leaning forward towards the window. Sections of the fence had been worn away so that the neighbours' yard was visible through the holes. I waited for a moment, watching as the man moved towards the house. He walked slowly and deliberately, glancing back towards the bush. A tattered curtain rippled lightly in the breeze in a window directly in front of me, a dark pane of glass between the two strips of fabric. Someone moved back and forth, a faint shadow between the strips. They paused for a moment and I wondered if I'd imagined it as I stood there briefly, before returning to Freya and Tyler's veranda.

Freya was near the fence, close to a passionfruit vine, the unripe skin of the fruit between the leaves. She bent over, her body strong and willowy. There was an odd ambiguity to her figure, a muscularity, that was not overtly feminine, and which strangely enough reminded me of Zac. Zac was like that too, thin and not overtly masculine, but not feminine either. It made me wonder if Zac's mother was like this and Tyler was attracted to androgynous women. I'd never met Zac's mother. She'd died when he was young. I watched Freya amongst the leaves and began thinking about her relationship with Zac, how she'd always been close to him, sometimes taking his side against Tyler.

A faint cry drifted over from the neighbours' and Freya glanced up, brushing her hand across her forehead. She looked anxious for a moment, before returning to her gardening. The leaves fanned outward, camouflaging part of her body. I could see the orange of her shirt amongst the plants. She moved carefully amongst the foliage and I glanced back and noticed a woodpile behind a gap in the fence next door.

I walked down to the garden, towards the outstretched arms of a tree. A horse was tethered loosely to another tree in the neighbours' yard and I remembered the wooden horse in the living room that had once belonged to Alison. It was interesting that Freya had kept it.

Freya had a curious expression on her face when she glanced up, almost a hint of expectation, and I wondered what she was thinking as she began fiddling with some twine holding a tomato vine to a stake. She snipped off the fraying ends, tossing them behind her as the horse strained against the reins, trying to get away from the post.

The boy I'd seen earlier walked out onto the porch. It might have been him watching at the window between the strips of curtain. He walked down the steps to the yard and loosened the horse's reins, pulling the animal away from the tree, leading it down the side passage. Hooves clopped gently in the distance and Freya looked up for a moment, the bump of her pregnancy showing faintly against the fabric of her shirt, her dark jeans stretched tight against her hips.

There was a movement in the bush, the shape of something beyond the tree line, a rapid image darting amongst the bushes.

'It's probably one of Radic's dogs,' Freya called out.

A blurred shape, only faintly visible, moved quickly, further back. The image seemed to vanish and when I glanced at Freya she was frowning at me.

'Did you see it?'

She turned away from me towards the bush, looking faintly annoyed. 'It'll be Nero, Radic's dog. He makes a nuisance of himself with Jet.'

She walked towards the house and I followed her inside, bothered by the image in the trees. I noticed the vase on the table again. It was shaped like the trunk of a tree, patterns of vines twisted around the neck, the green glaze revealing a design of stems and plants. The vines were knotted, like the vines I'd seen in the etchings of old fairy tales.

'Zac did it,' Freya said. 'He's been doing some wonderful things. He's really changed, Sarah. I don't agree with Tyler that things aren't good with him.'

I studied the vase, wondering if that was the case or if it was just wishful thinking on Freya's part. He'd always been a strange boy, a seemingly innocent exterior masking something a little more complex.

She picked up the vase carefully, filling it with water, arranging the flowers in a criss-cross pattern.

The last time I'd seen Zac was at Liam's funeral. He was still slim but had developed a more supple and muscular build. There was a young woman with him, fair hair, high cheekbones, dressed in jeans and a black blouse. She seemed to hover at the back of the parlour, respectfully keeping her distance. Zac had treated me a little awkwardly, as if the entire business of death was confronting, and I'd been conscious that he'd left the funeral early.

I watched Freya as she pursed her lips. She was arranging the flowers and clicked her tongue when the stems became tangled, ruining the pattern she was creating.

'Tyler and I drove out to see Zac a week ago,' she said. 'He hadn't seen or heard from Lola for a while. The neighbours never liked him, never approved of his friendship with her. You remember Karin, the woman who died in the car accident, the one he was a bit obsessed with. They blamed Zac for her death. They were friends with her on the coast. There were rumours about him grabbing the wheel. It happened after you left. I think Liam tried to intervene.'

I heard a shuffling noise and Freya left the room. She was gone for a while and returned with Jet, who leapt up at her. Freya stood back precariously, balancing herself against the dog's outstretched paws. She pushed him back forcefully and he fell down in front of her. I noticed the way she seemed in command of the dog.

I remembered Nathan's comment that Jim McLauchlan thought Freya was 'high maintenance'. There was a group of men down here who didn't like assertive women, thought it was 'against nature', as one of them had said jokingly within earshot of Freya and me at the pub. They seemed to revert to a tribal misogyny when threatened.

Jet stared up at her as she bent down again and brushed her hand over the thick fur on his back. I watched her patting him. She looked contemplative as if she were musing about something.

'Lola has a boyfriend up the coast,' she said, glancing up at me. 'Tyler said he's hiding her. He's sure of it. They just don't want to accept it. The fact that she wanted to get away from them. You've seen what they're like.'

She had a similar expression on her face to the one she'd had when she was brushing the herbs around the table. I wondered what she was thinking as she balanced herself, squatting down near Jet, moving her other arm around in a graceful, almost balletic way.

'I saw these guys when I was in town. One of them said he'd been in jail for eighteen years. I was wondering if they were friends of the Lonegans, that family in the mountains, the ones who were supposed to be dealing ice.'

Freya seemed baffled for a moment. 'Tom Lonegan's dealing weed. I don't think they're dealing ice. Aden Lonegan's Jet's old owner. He's Tom's brother. I don't know if it was him you saw. Aden was in jail but only for five years, for assault. It was actually a friend of theirs who mistreated Jet. That's what we were told, anyway.'

She reached out and began stroking Jet under the chin. I noticed the slackness of the dog's jaw, the sharpness of his teeth and the drool around the black outline of his gums. Jet's tongue lolled in his mouth, his teeth hooked, a yellowy white, almost like shark's teeth. They were pointed against the dark fur of his jaw.

Feeling repulsed, I looked away as Freya stood up and moved over to the vase. It was almost a relief to look at the clean lines and green glaze.

'No, the guy at the Emporium was inside for eighteen years. He must have been in for murder. There was another guy I ran into in the forest. He told me to tell you to keep Jet away. Dark, longish hair, a dent or a scar on his face.'

I noticed her frowning.

'Aden's dark. It doesn't sound like him, though. Who knows who Radic has out there. There was a guy living out that way but he's gone. The guy who was in for eighteen years is probably some friend of Aden's.'

She looked away from me and moved over to the bench. I remembered Moon. It was the only time I'd seen Tyler show intense emotion. Even after Scarlett died, he'd been remarkably contained. Some people had commented on his distance, that he'd been more detached than Freya.

I glanced at Freya, who was arranging the flowers, almost like a painting. Jet stared up at her, watching intently.

'What do you think happened with Karin and the accident?'

'Zac can be volatile but he'd never do something like grab the wheel. That's the sort of thing that happens around here, things get out of hand and then a rumour's started. It's what happened with Tyler after Scarlett's death.'

Gentle music drifted from outside, a bass drone, an acoustic guitar and the mournful sounds of a flute. When I looked back, Jet's jaw was wide, tongue lolling between his teeth. I stood up and walked to the doorway. There was something on the track again, a shape caught in the light. It seemed to dart between the trees.

Freya glanced back towards the bush. 'There's that animal in the bush again. It must be one of Radic's dogs. He's got three dogs. They're like a pack. The black ones often come in close to our place. One of them's a Rottweiler, that's Nero. The other's a mastiff cross. A friend of Zac's is training them.'

'The man I saw on the track had a tan dog.'

Freya began sipping water from a cup at the sink. The tea she'd been making earlier had been abandoned. She bent over and picked up a ball from the floor, bouncing it hard against the surface. It sprang back at her and Jet rushed towards it. She hit the ball back again and Jet began panting heavily. He rushed up, grabbing it between his teeth, shaking his head from side to side. I noticed the sharpness of his teeth as he shook it, tearing into it, crunching the rubber.

'What did he say to you, the guy in the forest?' She was staring at me intently now.

'He just told me to tell you to keep Jet away.'

I noticed the tear visible near the side of her blouse and the way the tangerine colour contrasted with the blue of her eyes.

'I wondered if I reminded him of Liam. He seemed to recognise me.'

She began busying herself with something at the sink as Jet played with the ball. 'Liam was helping Lola with her reading. Maybe he met someone out there.' She bent down and unravelled some twine that she pulled out, strand by strand, from under the sink.

She seemed troubled and I glanced to my left at Tyler's boots in the laundry, not far from the shovel. Freya reached in further and pulled out some gloves. She left the kitchen and Jet followed her out onto the porch. He sat down, his head resting on his forelegs and paws, fur dusky in the fading afternoon light.

I walked outside and stared towards the bush. When I glanced back, Jet's jaw was slack, that striking hint of amber in his eyes. I wondered if Aden Lonegan's friend had used Jet as a whipping post. I could see it in his defensiveness, the agitation and sudden outbursts of aggression.

Freya was squatting down amongst the plants again, hidden by the fanned leaves, the orange of her shirt contrasting with the green of the foliage. She moved back and forth through the plants, snipping and cutting. Jet left the porch and ran towards her and I studied her for a moment before returning inside to my bedroom.

There was a string of crystal beads on the dresser, similar to the ones that Freya had given me once for my birthday. They were close to the cut-glass perfume bottle and I leant over and picked them up, threading them through my fingers, studying the twinkling lights of the stones. As I fiddled with the necklace, I thought of the melancholy set to Freya's mouth, her bitterness and resentment when she'd been talking about her birth mother. Freya didn't really trust people; brought you close, then pushed you away again. Tyler was her rock but that had shifted too after Scarlett had died. People had turned on him, spreading rumours, and in a way Freya had been caught up in it too.

I wondered if it had been a type of carelessness, leaving Scarlett with Tyler when he might have been drinking and not focusing properly, but then the coroner had decided it was SIDS. These things can be difficult to prove and if I were being honest, the thought had crossed my mind that Freya might have done something herself, even if it was by accident. She'd been a good stepmother with Zac, but once or twice

I'd seen her lose it. I'd been thinking about it since a friend told me that you could get psychosis with severe cases of postnatal depression. I thought of all the contradictions in her personality, the fluctuating closeness of our friendship. She could be warm and kind, a seeker, but there was a coldness to her sometimes, just as Nathan had said, as if she were guarding herself from hurt, a certain rote behaviour that she'd learnt, just to please or survive.

The front door slammed and I pulled myself up from the bed, listening to the sound of someone walking down the corridor, heavy footsteps near my door. I walked outside and silence dominated the hallway. I could see a light shining from the study and I walked slowly down the hallway as muffled tones drifted from Freya and Tyler's bedroom, a male voice, low and forceful, and then a higher-pitched female one. I followed the corridor towards the end and when I walked inside, I noticed the books in the corner again. Nothing could be heard down the hallway and I stared up at the quality of the leather and the silvery sheen of the instruments. The heavy beige folds of curtains at the window looked torn, like shredded pieces at the hem. It looked like an animal had torn them. Tyler had left Moon in the car once and the dog had ripped the upholstery in a desperate attempt to escape.

As I was examining the curtain, Freya walked in and I stood back, embarrassed that she'd found me there. She sat down on the chair at the desk and I shifted my position near the curtains. There was a steeliness in her gaze and I smiled back at her nervously.

She was about to say something when Tyler walked in. He went directly to the window, standing near the bookcase. Jet was beside him and he walked away and sidled up to Freya. She reached over and patted the dog and I noticed how she seemed to relax when she touched him.

Tyler was leaning back against the bookcase. 'The man in the forest, the one you saw when you were out walking, what did he say?'

'He just told me to tell you to keep Jet away.'

Tyler frowned as if he were trying to piece something together.

'Radic has people staying out there. People he knew from the coast. I don't know what he's up to.'

Freya picked up a cushion and held it close to her, hugging it as Tyler leant back against the bookcase.

'I might want to talk to Radic about Liam. He lived nearby and Radic knew him. I've been having doubts about the fire. I mean, whether it was an accident. I know the police looked into it, but Freya said Radic was resentful about Liam's influence on Lola.'

Tyler shifted his position. 'You won't get anything out of him. He'd be suspicious of you because of your connection with us.'

I could hear the anger in his voice and I gazed back at him, conscious that he was studying me. His expression shifted to something friendlier, more relaxed, but I felt uneasy.

'Do you want to come to the pub? Jeannie's singing.' He was watching me now, observing my reaction, and I moved forward from the curtain.

'Yeah, I'll come. I haven't seen Jeannie for ages.'

I glanced down at Jet, who seemed distracted as he stood next to Freya. Tyler left the room.

Freya looked at me nervously as she reached over to Jet. 'Don't take any notice of him. He's really on edge because of the new baby and what happened with Scarlett. Are you coming with us?'

I nodded and we left the room together. Freya continued to her room and I walked down to my bedroom, bothered by Tyler's behaviour. I changed into my black jeans and a red top that flattered my olive skin. My dark hair hung loose about my shoulders and I could see my resemblance to Liam in the mirror, the wide dark eyes, thick lashes and black hair. Liam's eyes seemed to stare back at me, except that his were more vulnerable, like our mother's, and I remembered Connor tracing his fingers around my eyebrows once, commenting that they were curved like a bow. I pulled my hair back, trying to shake the image. I looked like I'd lost weight. My face seemed sharper, more hollow, not the usual roundness in the cheeks, and again I looked more like Liam. I sat down, trying to shake that image of his body in the fire. It was unbearable but my mind kept returning to it.

Pulling myself up, I left the room. Freya and Tyler were waiting for me in the kitchen. Tyler's hair was brushed back, accentuating his forehead and the angular planes of his face, square jaw and full lips. For the first time, I noticed the colour of his eyes, a pale colour, green or hazel.

'Are you coming? We were just coming to get you.'

I nodded and watched as Freya bent down and adjusted her shoes. She was wearing a long black dress, lacy at the edges, silvery earrings and a necklace.

Jet was outside on the porch as we left the house. His head was resting on his forelegs and paws, the same position I'd noticed earlier.

Tyler walked ahead of us. He was still distracted and I sensed that he wished he hadn't commented earlier about Radic. He opened the door to the car and glanced back at the house again.

I noticed the neighbours' front door set back from the porch. It was slightly ajar. I climbed into the back seat.

Tyler hesitated for a moment. Then he climbed in and turned on the ignition. We began driving along the dirt road, a thin sliver of moon visible in the sky, silvery against the inky darkness.

I wondered if Connor would be at the pub. The first time I'd ever seen him was when he was working as a fire-eater in town. He was dressed in a black turban and wide Arabian trousers. A stuffed cobra lay coiled on the edge of a platform as he stripped down to a black loincloth, lying down gradually on a bed of nails. Dents on his back had been visible when he uncoiled himself, leaping to his feet and immersing a torch in lighter fluid. He'd lit the torch, sprinkling more lighter fluid in his mouth, placing the torch close to his face, the flame shooting out as a roaring jet of fire. Connor's hair had been closely shaved against his scalp, his skin burnt a deep mahogany brown from a trip to Indonesia, a silver band around his wrist.

A tiny sprinkling of stars twinkled in the night sky as we drove into town, the fading sandstone walls of the pub in the distance.

Tyler pulled up outside and as I climbed out onto the street, I could see the alleyway in the distance where I'd seen that strange poster of the boy on the wall all those years ago, the one with the mobile phone number.

There was a group of men at the entrance to the pub, and I felt a sudden surge of loneliness as we walked towards them. One of them had a craggy face, deeply lined eyes, and I recognised him as Greg, a friend of Connor's, who he worked with at building sites, the one Freya had said they were thinking of going into business with. He nodded at me as we approached and I smiled back at him.

The familiar dark wooden tables were to my left when we walked inside, a stage with looped red folds of curtains. Jeannie shimmied onto the stage, her voluptuous figure draped in a black dress clinging to her body, the curves of her stomach and rounded bottom visible through the sheer fabric. She began singing a gutsy style of blues like Janis Joplin and I noticed an old friend of Liam's playing bass.

Freya was holding back, not joining Tyler at the bar. She seemed tense and was biting her lip. 'Darcy's coming tomorrow.' She glanced over at Tyler. 'I decided to have her down. Tyler's been talking about taking her up the coast to Fingal's Beach. He thinks it'll be better, away from here. It might be more relaxed.'

'Your birth mother?'

'Yeah.'

I remembered the rock platform and the cliffs descending to the sand, not as steep as Black Mountain but still precarious. I'd been there a few times with Connor.

'It's quite wild up there. I'm not sure Darcy will like it but I think it's a good idea to get away.'

She looked away from me towards Tyler. A woman was talking to him, petite and fair, high cheekbones and angular face. They were bent closely towards each other. She looked like the girl with Zac at Liam's funeral.

Freya was frowning at her. 'It's Ava, Lola's sister. I think he's talking to her about Lola.'

I could see Ava in profile but her expression wasn't clear, only the tension in her body. An older man came to join them, sandy-haired, slim build. He seemed to lean protectively towards her. She was wearing a dress made of a patterned fabric, like leopard skin. I watched her pick up a lighter from the bar, flicking it on and off, fiddling with it nervously. Tyler's jaw looked clenched as he shifted his position. He was leaning towards them, talking intently and Freya was studying him. I noticed Ava glance back towards us and Freya frowned at her. She walked towards them and touched Tyler on the arm as Ava stepped back a little.

Tyler's face was rigid, his muscles tense. Freya was talking to him, then she turned and began walking back towards me. She walked a little ahead as Tyler caught up and put his arm around her. He seemed to hold on to her in an odd way.

'It's nothing,' Tyler said when he saw my expression. 'We were talking to them about Zac. Critchett's targeting him. That's who Ava's talking to.'

I tried to gauge what he was thinking, how worried he was. Freya glanced at Tyler and began walking towards the bistro.

'I was thinking of seeing my father,' I said, as I caught up to her. 'He lives inland from the coast now. People say he's a different man.'

Ava was standing with Critchett, the man who'd been hovering over her protectively when she was talking to Tyler.

'I used to work with Dave Critchett,' Freya said. 'He's an OK guy. He's respectful towards women.'

Freya was looking in the direction of the other room. She smiled faintly as we ordered and walked over to a table near the door. She sat down and began playing with a bread roll, glancing through the doorway at Critchett and Ava. 'So, you're thinking of seeing your father? How do you feel about that?'

'Nervous, I guess. Liam told me he wanted to talk to him about something but I don't know what it was. Someone he saw. Do you know anything about it?'

'No, he didn't mention anything.' She was staring at Ava and Critchett again. She seemed unhappy, as if something wasn't right. 'Your parents' relationship was very fraught, wasn't it? That's what Liam said. He talked about your father but he said your mother could be difficult. I remember you mentioned it. He said she shopped him up to their dealer and he took a beating for it.'

I stared at her, wondering what she was getting at. 'Yes, but there was a background of domestic violence. She did it deliberately to get him away from her.'

I wondered why she was so sympathetic to my father when she'd been critical of him in the past.

There was another man talking with Ava now, tall, good-looking, wavy dark hair.

'That's Aden Lonegan,' Freya said. 'Jet's old owner. Is he the man you saw in the forest?'

'No, the other man's hair was longer. He seemed older, darker.'

Freya was frowning. It was obvious Ava was enjoying Aden's company.

'He can be quite charming when he wants to be. He's not stupid. Radic's other friends are more difficult.'

Jeannie returned to the stage. I sat back in my chair and noticed Aden walk towards a back room with Ava. They disappeared through a doorway. Jeannie was singing an old jazz classic, 'Summertime'.

Freya had that melancholy expression again and I smiled at her, wondering what she was thinking.

'Remember when you and Liam were talking about starting a band?' she said. 'You were both really talented musicians, like your parents, Liam especially.' She looked upset when she mentioned Liam.

Tyler pulled out his chair and was facing the stage, studying Jeannie as she sashayed along in front of the crowd.

Our meals arrived and Freya wrapped her pasta skilfully around the metal prongs. I noticed the sharpness of the metal as she jabbed at a tomato, the finicky way she fiddled with it. She glanced across at a group milling around the bar. One of them had longish hair like one of the ex-cons at the Emporium.

Freya glanced back at Tyler, who was studying them. I noticed the man I'd seen earlier in the neighbours' yard, the one who was wearing a jacket with the circular red transfer. He was at the back of the group and when I looked back at Tyler, he was watching him.

*

Around midnight, we left the pub. Freya was talking about Liam, how they used to have long conversations together, how she missed him. That odd sense of detachment took hold, the same feeling I'd had on the beach. When I turned, I noticed Critchett following us. He quickened his pace, almost sprinting, his long legs gaining ground. Tyler pulled back and began speaking to him as Freya and I reached the car. I saw Tyler nodding as Freya and I stood there waiting for him, then he walked back towards us. Critchett remained stock-still for a moment, staring back. He appeared to look towards Freya, who frowned and glanced away. Tyler couldn't see him and when I glanced at Freya, she seemed to be distancing herself from him. I wondered how well she knew Critchett.

Freya unlocked the door and I climbed in.

'How do you know this Critchett guy?'

'I worked with him at the Blue Rider.'

'That café on the coast?'

'Yeah, it was a while ago.'

Tyler climbed into the passenger seat and Freya started the car.

'I don't like what they're doing,' said Tyler. 'They're targeting Zac.'

Freya's eyes were visible in the mirror and I watched her for a moment, before staring out into the darkness. She looked focused but there was a harshness in her gaze as she began driving along the highway.

A road sign flashed up ahead in the headlights, and I noticed the quick movement of a possum or kangaroo caught in the light and then the track where I'd emerged from the bush onto the road after I'd seen the man on the path. Lines of trees whizzed past, skirting the highway, glimpses of trails that led further into the bush.

I glanced at Freya in the mirror again.

Tyler began talking about his work, how he'd probably be laid off soon from the park but he might get some work from Doug. 'I've still got three days,' he said. 'I don't know what I'm going to do after that but Doug might help.'

We drove for some time, Tyler talking about how angry he was with the neighbours.

Freya turned off the highway and began driving along the dirt road.

She parked the car outside and I glanced over at the neighbours' yard. I noticed a troubled expression on Tyler's face as we climbed out, but Freya looked more composed as we walked towards the house. There were no lights on next door and the windows were completely black, so they must have gone into town.

Tyler paused at the door for a moment and seemed wary, as if someone or something might be lying in wait for him. Opening the door slowly, he stepped into the hallway. There was a light on in the study. Someone must have left it on and Tyler looked anxious as he walked past.

I followed the corridor and as I walked into my bedroom, I could hear arguing from the hallway. I stared out towards the yard, expecting to see Jet. The perfume bottle sat on the dresser, the facets of the glass shining in the light. There was a doll nearby on a chair and I studied its rounded arms and flat chest, remembering that Freya had planned to give it to Scarlett, so perhaps she was thinking of giving it to the upcoming child. The room was probably intended as a nursery. The doll stared back at me and I felt uncomfortable as I glanced up at a pattern of shadows on the wall, remembering an owl that had flown into the house when I was a child, how it had flapped its wings and bashed against the walls. I studied the shadows in the darkness thinking of the owl, its eyes wide in the dark, terrified and knowing, beating its wings helplessly.

I got ready for bed and lay down, feeling unsettled as I drifted off to sleep. The hours were broken by nightmares, a bird flapping constantly, its large wings in tatters, voluminous black eyes.

When I awoke, light was streaming in between the curtains and I turned away, glancing up at the window. I'd closed the door in the night but the glass perfume bottle was turned slightly. Trying to recall if I'd knocked it, I climbed out of bed and got dressed. Leaving the room, I passed by the living room, remembering the ripped curtains in the study. I wondered if Jet had been locked inside, panicked, and tried to scratch his way out, just as Moon had in the car once when Tyler had locked him in. Freya had told him how careless he was, that she couldn't believe he didn't realise it. There had been anger in her voice and she'd spoken with a hostility that had surprised me.

When I walked into the kitchen, Freya was standing near the bench. She moved over to the table, avoiding my gaze, and poured some tea.

Tyler walked in. He made some coffee and was scowling as he lifted the cup. I noticed the lean angular lines of his face, and the stubble on his chin. He still looked good in spite of his age and I remembered Freya's stories when they were first together, that he was better in bed than most of the young men she'd had sex with.

'I'm not sure what they're up to,' Tyler said, studying me impassively. 'The neighbours are in some sort of alliance with Critchett and the Lonegans. I don't know what's going on.' He took a sip of coffee and moved closer to the bench.

Freya seemed to be studying him and he stared back at her. I was surprised at her expression, angry and a little contemptuous.

'Dave's OK,' she said. 'Aden's probably keeping his distance too. It's true Radic has it in for you with Zac's relationship with Lola but you should just leave it alone.'

He glanced over at me, ignoring her. 'It's a long journey up the coast, Sarah. Are you sure you want to come with us when we take Darcy? You got seasick that time we went out on Doug's boat.'

'Yeah, I'll be OK.'

I was bothered by the way Freya avoided eye contact. She appeared to be thinking and raised the cup to her lips.

Tyler walked out to the porch.

'I'm sorry he's so difficult,' said Freya. 'It hasn't been easy in the last few years.' She was watching him through the doorway.

I detected that feeling of distrust again, like that time she'd said goodbye to me at the bus stop and the strange comment she'd made about me being her conscience.

She walked over to the fridge, pulling out some juice, a loaf of bread and cereal, bringing them over to the table.

I made myself some breakfast, homemade bread and jam, thick creamy yoghurt and fruit, conscious that Freya had become very quiet. I noticed her eyes cloud over and I began to feel uneasy again.

'His moodiness has really got a lot to do with Zac and the baby,' she said. 'Issues with him being a parent, general stress. Don't take him too seriously. He was looking forward to you coming down. It won't be that bad with Darcy.'

I nodded, feeling uncomfortable.

'Are you going to see Ivy?' she asked. 'It's quite a while since she and Liam broke up. She mentioned you were going to see her.'

'I might see her today, Connor too. I want to ask them about Liam.'

'You can take my car if you like. We can use Tyler's car.' She reached into her pocket and handed me her car keys.

I watched her pull some jam towards her and begin spooning it onto the toast and I thought I caught something distant in her eyes.

'It's a shame that you and Liam drifted apart. He often spoke about it.'

There was a hint of criticism in her tone and it made me defensive. Freya had said herself that she and Tyler hadn't had that much to do with Liam just before his death. She'd insisted his death was an accident, everyone had said that. I glanced at her, knowing that she thought I was reading too much into it.

Freya took a bite of her toast. She looked contemplative now, concentrating on a magazine beside her. I sensed she'd withdrawn into herself and stood up, feeling uneasy. I walked to the window, studying the bush. Turning back to the green vase on the table, I walked over and touched the ornate pattern on the side, remembering Zac's fascination with the forest, the way he used to walk for hours in the bush. Freya was reading the magazine and I sensed she was holding back about something.

Deciding it was best to see Ivy, I left the room. Passing by their bedroom, I noticed some of Tyler's clothes on the bed. They were spread out across the surface. He had a way of making his presence felt. The clothes seemed to dominate the doona. The curtains were drawn as usual and I wondered if it had become a habit, pulling them across to block out the neighbours. There was a painting on the wall depicting a rural setting, a village with block-shaped houses made of solid stone that reminded me of my grandparents' village in Italy. I noticed Zac's signature in the corner and wondered if Liam had shown him a photo of the scene. They'd been close in the old days, two young men who had lost their mothers. Zac's mother had died of cancer when he was young. The painting was the main focus, taking you away from the window, or any likely view outside. It had a calming effect. There was a bridge in the corner made of stones in an arc shape, similar to a bridge I'd seen once in Italy.

Freya's make-up was on the dressing table, black clothing on the chair. Sometimes she used to rim her eyes with kohl, her pale skin powdered with its light dusting of freckles. Zac had looked up to her, when he was young, as someone who could calm him down when he was most distressed, a person who gave him a sense of guidance.

I walked down to my bedroom, thinking about Freya, her nurturing side, the contradictions in her personality. The perfume bottle made me uncomfortable as I stared at it, noticing the position near the bed. Ivy commented once that Tyler didn't like phoney-looking women and that Darcy was like that. She said Tyler thought fragile and vulnerable people were OK. He didn't mind if they were knocked down in life but kept trying to pick themselves up. He admired people like that but apparently Tyler thought Darcy was weak.

I studied the doll in the corner, thinking about Tyler and his attitude to women, how he seemed to admire strength in them while at the same time not wanting them to have too much control. He'd made some comment about me and Connor once, how I expected too much, and how I didn't understand Connor, because of my own background. He said I'd never gotten over my father's behaviour and my mother's death. We'd argued about it, Tyler saying that I was constantly looking for evidence of betrayal, forever on the alert, scrutinising and noticing things that didn't exist.

There was a clutter of papers on the desk in the study as I passed by, uncharacteristically disordered for Freya and Tyler. The leather chair was askew, and more papers were scattered about. I walked inside and flipped through them quickly, thinking about Tyler and how I often didn't agree with him. There were bills, articles on horticulture, some large documents about delisting acreage in parks. I glanced up at the bookshelves and noticed there were gaps. Leaning back against the desk, I wondered about Tyler's grandfather and the books and instruments. They looked like the sort of thing a doctor would use. Alison had mentioned once that Tyler's father was in the army and she might have said his grandfather was a scientist.

There was a vase, gold and orange, waving palm trees. It looked like one of those scenes from North Africa, colonial times.

A dog barked and plates clattered down the hallway. I stood up slowly and left the room, walking outside to the garage, where I struggled with the garage door. Old sculptures and bags of materials were stacked up against the back, cobwebs, gardening implements.

I heard a shuffling noise outside and my heart began to pound as I glanced down at a damaged piece of crockery on the floor, shining in the light. It looked burnt and I imagined the light of the fire in Liam's house, his body destroyed by the flames. There'd been no evidence of arson, the police had said, only that he'd been smoking in bed and he'd been drinking very heavily. There was also no sign he'd tried to escape, and his body had been burnt beyond recognition. No cause of death had been established other than the fire.

Trying to calm myself, I noticed a clutter of objects at the back of the garage. They'd been pushed up against the wall, wooden sculptures piled on top of one another, blank faces, like the defaced images of Puritan statues. Brightly coloured buttons sat on a bench assembled in neat rows, a parka and jeans on the floor, things that made no sense to me. Perhaps they were objects Tyler was intending to use for his sculptures.

A collection of worn sheets and army blankets were piled in the corner, a small dusty window, like frosted glass, with a pattern like finger marks. I remembered my father's shed, how I'd drawn traces in the dust as a child after I'd been banished there for some misdemeanour, the punishment out of proportion to the crime. On a dirty collection of blankets, I noticed the imprint of a shape.

Backing away, I climbed into the car, reversing it out of the garage, and when I turned to my right, a dog was standing in the bushes. It bolted towards me, a collar with pointed studs around its neck, silver glinting against black fur. It charged at me as I accelerated. Breathing deeply, I pressed my foot on the accelerator.

As I drove quickly, the road veered steeply through the mountain range. Dense trees, thick with gnarled roots, lined the road, lone trunks emerging above the canopy. There was a lake up ahead, twisted forests on the lee of the mountain, ghostly skeletal branches. It reminded me of the approach of winter, the depressing greyness and cold, and my flight away from here; then the transition from dark, heavy forests and skies into a rocky arid landscape of golden light. The sense of isolation and beauty was alternately uplifting and depressing, forests thick and impenetrable.

A man in a road gang dressed in bright orange plastic held up his finger, gesturing 'up yours'.

Boredom began to take hold and I turned on the radio. A desultory service station came into view, and I began to feel an uncomfortable conjuncture of my past and present selves, like haunting shadows eclipsing the sun, the different lives I'd led, the identities I'd discarded like the casings of moths.

I noticed a pale light and a large bird taking flight beyond the branches and an overpowering melancholy took hold, dominating my thoughts. I could almost hear my mother's voice through the darkness, memories of walking across paddocks and through trees. She was standing at the edge of the bush, not daring to set foot on the path, frightened that my father might chase her amongst the hazards of sticks and stones. Her voice was overpowering now, dominating my thoughts. I remembered running after her when she'd been the victim of one of my father's assaults. She'd staggered along the path not wanting any help. She didn't want to put me to the trouble and had stood there stoic but wary, unable to see the path through the trees.

A massive drop dipped into a valley and I noticed Ivy's place up ahead. It was wooden, and broken down, the roof bolted across with planks, patches of sunlight between the branches.

There was another ramshackle house nearby and I climbed out of the car and walked to the door. I rang the doorbell and after a few moments, Ivy appeared, small and elfin, dark hair sculptured in a short cut around her face. She was wearing a necklace, a silver chain of red gems, like the crystal chain on the dresser at Freya's. There was a brooch with a design like a lyre near the shoulder of her top. I imagined her dancing in the nightclubs of New York, where she'd lived for a time. Her body was like that of a young boy, lithe and graceful.

She leant forward and embraced me, leading me into the living room, where several well placed photographs stood on the mantelpiece. They were all in gilt-edged frames. One was of a man who had been photographed from the waist up, dark and emaciated. It was an old-fashioned portrait that must have been taken in a photographic studio, because there were no objects in the room and the man appeared to float like a ghost, insignificant and powerless in relation to the surrounding physical space.

'It's my grandfather,' Ivy said. She'd told me once that her great grandparents were Russian. It was during the Communist era and her grandmother had fallen in love with a boy of White Russian descent whose parents had rejected her. Ivy gazed back at me.

She moved away from the photo and I followed her through to the kitchen, where she began busying herself, pulling out a canister from the cupboard. I recognised the methods of distraction.

'It's difficult processing it all,' she said at last. 'Liam's death, I mean. I suppose Freya told you Lola's up the coast with her boyfriend. People thought Liam had something to do with her leaving but it's not true. I've seen her boyfriend and she's not there.' She moved over to the kettle, her back to me.

I noticed a room to my left, lit faintly by the pale spring sun. Ivy had been suspicious of Freya, had thought she was interested in Liam, but then Freya had denied it. She said Ivy overreacted to things.

She turned to face me. The jewellery she was wearing glinted in the light, earrings shaped like a spiral shell, gold bracelets and rings. Her tight black jeans and tunic top with its bold geometric designs flattered the spare lines of her body. 'It's possible she's with Aden Lonegan,' she said. 'Lola and Ava are very friendly with him, so was Freya for a while. She worked with a friend of his, Dave Critchett.'

There was a painting of two girls on the wall in front of me. They were on a landing with a sunflower. The flower dominated the landing in a menacing way and one of the girls stood before it, her hair standing on end, drifting towards the ceiling. The other girl was close to one of the doors, her chest exposed as she faced the other way.

'I don't know if Liam met someone out there at Radic's and he upset them,' Ivy said. 'I just think it's a distraction, all this talk about Liam and the neighbours. Liam had nothing to do with Lola leaving. She's capable of making up her own mind. She's a strong girl. She was a bit in awe of Aden Lonegan, Ava too. Maybe they're hiding her.' She pulled out some milk and brought it over to the table.

'Aden was at the pub last night. He was with Ava and Dave Critchett. Tyler said something about him and the Lonegans being in alliance with the neighbours.'

Ivy looked at me sceptically. 'I'm not sure what he means by that. No one's in an alliance. He makes a big deal about nothing.'

'Do you think Zac knows where she is?'

She studied me thoughtfully. 'He had a relationship with her but I don't think he's been in contact. Freya and Tyler didn't like his involvement with her. I think Freya knows more than she's saying.' She sat down and poured the tea, glancing across at me.

I remembered Freya's behaviour the night before, her glances with Critchett and Ava.

'Freya's birth mother's coming down,' Ivy said, stirring her tea. 'You remember how it was with Scarlett. It'll probably bring it all back.'

I sensed something unpleasant in her tone, a hint of criticism towards Freya.

She reached over to a jar of biscuits. They were knobbly with clusters of nuts and raisins, the kind of biscuits she used to make when she lived on the coast with Liam. I could smell the roasted peanuts, the rich aromatic scent, and I took one and broke off one of the nuts. Liquid seeped out around the saucer of my cup.

'What happened with her birth mother? She never talks about her. She said she can't remember much but I remember you met her.'

'I only met her when Freya contacted her years ago. I felt she blamed Freya for everything, even her own unhappiness. I only found out recently and accidentally, but Freya was blamed for the death of a child. The girl fell downstairs when Freya was supposed to be looking after her and her stepfather blamed her. She was very young. Matt, the psychologist, told me she can't remember anything. It only came out after you left, accidentally really, and she hasn't spoken to anyone about it.'

I thought of my mother, how she sometimes took my father's side. I remembered Freya's comments the previous night about my mother's death, how she seemed to be looking for excuses for it, implying that she'd somehow brought the situation on herself, had deserved someone like my father.

'Freya's never mentioned it, about the child who fell downstairs, I mean.'

Ivy picked up her cup again and held it tightly. I sensed that feeling again, an antagonism towards Freya.

'It only came out recently. I think Darcy and the girl's father realised she wasn't to blame. I didn't like Darcy, actually. I thought she was one of those women who don't like other women. Freya told me she didn't want to see her. I'm surprised she's changed her mind. I think Darcy felt guilty about her.'

I leant forward in my seat, adjusting my position, curious about Darcy. My tea was lukewarm now and a piece of nut cut sharp against my tongue. I studied Ivy, thinking about my mother's difficult behaviour, how in spite of being a war hero and a loving husband, my grandfather had been a strict and sometimes punitive father. It hadn't all been black and white. She'd reacted off her parents, had been attracted to my father as a rebel who'd seemed dangerous and interesting.

'Darcy's an unusual name.'

'She's not that unusual. Well dressed, bourgeois, that's what she's become but not what she was.'

Freya kept you at arm's length and I wondered if Darcy was the same, distancing herself. Freya's coldness was more a defence mechanism and a cover for a deeper insecurity.

I glanced outside and noticed a man in the yard, talking to a young girl. He leant towards her in a fatherly way. She was hitting a golf ball into the air and I watched the white ball spinning in an arc across the yard.

Ivy smiled at them benevolently. 'They're friends and neighbours.' She glanced back towards the kitchen. 'People said Freya was losing it after Scarlett. I thought she was depressed and frightened. She's always been guarded, Tyler too. She mentioned your father recently. She said Liam had been thinking of reconciling with him.'

'I've been thinking of seeing him too. Liam told me he wanted to talk to him about something.'

'He said something to me about that too, but I don't know what it was.'

She walked out to the yard and I followed her. There were tiered slopes leading down towards the undergrowth. I noticed a cat, black fur, yellow eyes. It moved towards her, a little reserved as she coaxed it over. I watched it rub against her leg, tail moving back and forth like a pendulum. She picked it up and walked back inside. I followed her and sat down at the table again.

There were bits of paper on the bench and I glanced up at the canisters on the shelf, a bit more disordered than Freya's kitchen. A dish with milk sat in the corner near the door. It looked like it had curdled slightly and I wondered if Ivy had been away, or had let things go a bit like Liam.

Ivy stroked the cat. I looked to my left, noticing a red light, a candle like a burning sun, and then out to the garden, branches, thick and ugly. When I glanced back, Ivy was studying me and I realised I must have looked distracted or distressed. I could smell perfume like patchouli oil. It reminded me of Freya's perfume bottle and the scent in my mother's dresses, the night the owl had flown into the attic, flapping its wings as it bashed against the walls.

Ivy tickled the cat under the chin. 'You shouldn't listen to what Freya and Tyler say about Radic,' she said. 'He's OK. He's not how he seems. They used to work together at the park. There were arguments about the development. Radic wanted it. He thought it would bring more work. Tyler was against it. Radic changed back and forth. First he was for it, then he wasn't.'

I noticed reflections in the glass above me, a mirror on the wall, and I began to feel unsteady, dizzy almost. 'Arguments?'

'Oh, just about delisting acreage, but it's all over. There's not going to be a development, only on the coast. Their dispute is really about Lola.'

A moth flickered and a shadow crept across the corner of the room.

Ivy was standing a little away from me. 'It's strange when adults are jealous of other adults when it comes to children, don't you think? I mean with Darcy not wanting to see Alison, and Matt the psychologist. Tyler's jealous of him. Freya does some work for him, some gardening.'

I watched her closely, thinking there was nothing in her reaction that suggested anything untoward about Freya's relationship with Matt.

Ivy walked outside again and I followed her towards the rows of vegetables, pumpkin and potatoes, apple and peach trees at the back. We walked along the tiered slope that backed away towards the bush. Further along the slope, I noticed the side of the house next door, wooden planks splintered near the bush.

Ivy was still standing a little away from me, framed by the trees, and I listened to a crow as I glanced up towards the blurred wings of a bird near the treetops.

We strolled back inside and talked for a while longer, then she walked with me to the car. I felt more confident as she leant towards me, embracing me, the warmth of her arms.

'Be careful,' she said.

I climbed into the car and began driving along the highway, thinking about the chaotic lives Liam and I had led as children, the people we'd been subjected to. Liam had tried to protect me, had borne the brunt of our father's temper, and I'd felt guilty about it even though I was younger. Connor had said Liam had been drinking more, experiencing flashes of anger, arguing with people. It was true, he took people on, particularly if he thought they were wrong about something.

There was a fork in the road and I took the left one that wound down towards the coast. I began thinking about Tyler's jealousy, his insecurity about Freya. It reminded me of my father, the confidence that seemed to dissolve in the face of perceived threat, the lashing out under stress.

I drove for some time, staring out in the distance, dark clouds on the horizon. Further on, I could see the grey of the ocean, merging into a pale green, the lacy outline of the surf.

Fishing boats were clustered around wharves as I reached the outskirts of town, their masts at odd angles, pushed forward by the wind. It was warmer than the day before.

Connor usually swam in all weather, rain or shine. He'd sounded a little distant when I'd rung him before I came down, but at the same time pleased I was coming. I thought about the Polish woman Freya had mentioned. The one he'd had a relationship with. He'd had a chequered history with relationships. Both of us were similar that way. His secretiveness had undermined trust.

I drove on past white houses with slate-coloured rooves. The protected inlet led out towards the sea, a trawler moored at the marina, a blue hull with a chrome band, and a mast leaning out from the prow. Doug, Tyler's friend, who worked at the marina further north, had taken us up the coast, where Tyler wanted to take Darcy. The waves had risen up over the boat as they'd hauled in fish and I'd felt sick as I watched the fish die.

Driving through town, I passed the pub with its white wooden railing, a long white building with a colonnade and an upper balcony looking out towards the pier. Connor's house was set back from the road, a few kilometres out of town. It was next to a reserve and the owner had erected a sign, 'Private Property Keep Out'. There were kentia palms in bronze pots and a dog barked, low and hollow, as a group of youths loitered in a reserve across the road. Shrieks drifted down from a balcony, a woman chastising a child.

After parking the car, I glanced across to the flats next door. A girl was standing on the upstairs balcony, her hair lank and black. She had a slovenly look, pale olive skin, similar to my own. An older woman came to join her. They had a similar appearance, fine features, hollow sharp cheekbones. Even from a distance, the woman's eyes looked tired her long arms were more muscular than I'd seen on a woman. There was a cockiness in her manner as she gazed down at me.

I climbed out of the car and walked towards Connor's place, where I rang the doorbell.

I hadn't seen him for a while. He'd been away in Indonesia and had missed Liam's funeral and when he answered the door I noticed his hair was cropped against his scalp. It looked similar to the time I'd first met him when he worked as a fire-eater, the familiar eyebrows, full lower lip, long straight nose. The tattoos down his left arm were clearly visible below his shirt, a fish and a treble clef.

There was something contained in his movements as we walked inside, a tension that made me uneasy. He sat down and slouched back into the cushions on the couch. Patches were visible on the fabric. It looked like the covering of a moulting animal. Connor's body appeared tense like a spring as he leant back into the cushions. Tyler was like that too, a physicality and containment, except that Connor's body was more athletic, wiry and taller, more agile like a cat. I remembered the muscular lines of his back, and the curves of the muscles and sinews in his arms, my palms and fingers grazing his legs, the touch of his hands in the night.

Connor shifted his position on the couch and leant forward towards the table, picking up a pouch of tobacco.

'I've just come from Ivy's.'

He glanced up at me and I watched him fiddle with the tobacco. I waited for him to speak but he didn't say anything. I could sense the anxiety in my chest and was conscious that I was breathing shallowly.

'Freya's been evasive since I've been out there,' I said, watching him crumble the tobacco. 'Did Liam say anything to you about a car following him? I don't think he was paranoid. I've been having doubts about the fire, whether it was deliberately lit.'

Connor leant back against the couch and shifted his position. 'I think Liam's death was an accident, Sarah. You know how he got when he was smoking weed. He was depressed too. Your father coming out of jail brought back memories. As for Freya, she's always had that manner, evasive, distracted, whatever you want to call it.'

'You said Liam had tried ice. Maybe that explains the hallucinations.'

Connor frowned as he fiddled with the tobacco. 'He only tried it once or twice. I don't really know what was going on. I think he got it from out of town.'

I could hear the tension in his voice as he reached over for his papers. He clenched his hand, a powerful hand that was used to clutching a trapeze. He began rolling a cigarette and I watched him lick the paper, sealing it.

'Liam wanted to see Dad. Do you know anything about it, something about a guy he met?'

'I heard there was a guy from out of town. I think he's a friend of Julie's, that lady your father had a relationship with. It might be something to do with Tyler.'

'Tyler?'

'Yeah, but I don't know what it was about. Liam didn't want to talk about it.' He lit the cigarette and inhaled, blowing smoke away from me. 'Your father lies, you know. You can't trust him. I'd be careful if you're speaking with him.'

He had a serious expression on his face and I watched as he leant back against the couch. It was true, my father did lie, anything to get out of a difficult situation, or worse.

'Ivy just told me about a kid who died. Freya was supposed to be watching her. It must have been traumatic because she's never mentioned it. Her father thought it was Freya's fault and for some reason her birth mother believed him.'

I felt uncomfortable, thinking about my mother's allegiance to my father again, the way she always took his side when Liam and I reacted against him. I watched Connor lean forward to the ashtray. He looked surprised.

'She's never spoken about it to me. I think she cut off ties with her birth mother.'

'You never know the truth with Freya, don't you think? A bit like my father.'

Connor inhaled deeply, slouching back further into the couch. The ashtray was made of blue glass.

He shifted back against the cushions, looking contemplative. 'You never used to think that way about her, but, yeah, I know what you mean. I was surprised they got back together after Scarlett's death. Maybe the new baby will take their minds off it.'

'So you know about the baby?'

'Tyler told me. He didn't seem all that happy, like he wasn't prepared for it. I suppose he's happy. He just hasn't processed what happened with Scarlett.' He was watching me and looked guarded as if he were about to tell me something, possibly about Tyler, but then he seemed to back off. 'Anyway, it's been getting them down, all this stuff about Lola. I spoke to Tyler about it. He told me the neighbours are focusing on Zac. They think he knows something.'

'What do you think?'

He shrugged. 'Maybe. He's still pretty fucked up. She's probably out there with him, or someone he knows. Maybe Aden.'

He left the couch and walked into the bedroom, where he pulled out some swimming gear from the drawer. 'Do you want to go to the beach?'

I walked in and he handed me some board shorts and a T-shirt. I changed into them and we left the house, walking out into the courtyard, where I noticed the two women I'd seen next door in the yard. Connor smiled at them.

'Who are they?'

'Bernice and Lili. They're friends of the Lonegans.'

I glanced back at them as we crossed the road to the reserve. Stones scuttled as we climbed a hill, yellow earth, dry and powdery, a pale watery blue sky. It reminded me of the aerial paintings that Tyler did in his shed inspired by what he thought was the view from above. Connor was a little ahead of me as I puffed up the hill. He pulled back and stopped for a moment, waiting for me. I noticed the tattoo on his arm again, the blue ink of the fish and the treble clef.

'I saw some strange stuff in Tyler's shed, bedclothes, like someone had been sleeping there, weird sculptures, like he used to do.'

'Jet was sleeping in the shed when they first took him on. Some of the stuff's probably Zac's. He takes advantage of them, leaving it there. He's a hoarder, like Tyler.'

We continued climbing until we reached the ridge that led to the sea. Connor stooped down to pick up a piece of stone on the path. He looked up at the ridge and I glanced down at the damaged casings and shells of insects on the path. Connor threw the stone down and I gazed out towards the beach, surf rolling onto the shore. There were distant figures near the shoreline, a young man running along the beach, arms swinging rhythmically by his sides.

Connor was standing to my right, studying the surf. Someone was out in the breakers. They plunged beneath the waves, disappearing beneath the swell. I had that odd feeling of someone watching that I'd had back at Freya and Tyler's house and there was a troubled expression on Connor's face when I glanced up at him. We walked down the hill towards the shore.

There were only two people on the beach as we reached the sand and I glanced to my right at a wide sweep of sand stretching like a pale mirage into the distance. Connor stripped down to his costume and ran towards the surf.

I stood there for a moment. There was no one near us on the beach but I thought I saw someone in the sandhills. I stripped down to my costume and began walking towards the surf. Plunging into the water, I pushed gently against the tide. I couldn't see Connor anywhere, only the figure further out in the distance on the sand. Dipping below the surface, my body pushed back against the currents.

Smoke drifted towards the sky and when I glanced back, I noticed the man on the shore again, disappearing towards the rise, seagulls careering overhead. I lay back in the water, the current pushing me, back and forth.

Pulling myself up, I swam back towards the shore. The man had gone and I walked back up the beach towards my towel. I had a sense of someone watching again and when I glanced back, Connor was nearby. He was looking back towards the hill.

'Did you see that guy over there?'

He was staring back. 'Sometimes people camp up there.'

He was probably thinking of the state I was in after my mother's death. I'd told him about it. It was years ago but I'd been frightened, had completely withdrawn, a sense of danger that never seemed to dissipate.

Spears of grass whipped against my ankles as we left the beach and I noticed a black slug contorting and shifting its way down my leg. I bent down and flicked it away.

'I was going to suggest you see Radic,' he said. 'But I'm not sure you should now. I'm worried you're not in a good state.'

The old arguments formulated in my mind about Connor being patronising, that he thought I was over-anxious, but I checked myself. He must have decided not to push it too as he began talking about the time he'd lived in the mountains, how he wanted to go back there.

'I'm going there later,' he said. 'To see some friends.'

We continued talking until we reached the road. He hesitated for a moment and glanced across towards the park. I had an odd sense that he was glad I was here, that he was trying to reach out. We reached the house and walked through to the kitchen.

I glanced through the doorway and noticed the woman from next door at the entranceway to the house. She was dark, her skin a pale olive, black hair, darker than mine. Her arms were folded and she seemed to be studying me as if she'd come to see why I was here.

Connor walked to the doorway. I could hear them speaking softly then he closed the door and walked to the fridge, where he pulled out a beer.

'What was that about?'

'Oh, nothing, just something about Zac. He's been bothering them.'

He leant forward. There was a feeling of distance now, something strained from the past, of trying to create a bridge when there wasn't one. He looked thinner, his hair a dark bluish black shadow on his scalp. The room was bright, a pale yellow, and he held up his hand when he began explaining about the carpentry he was doing. I glanced at the wide stretch of his fingers.

He looked away from me, stood up and walked to the sink, washing his hands. When he returned, he picked up a guitar, lounging back on the chair. The sound of chords filled the room, Connor's voice, drifting towards me. I remembered the sound of music from Freya and Tyler's neighbours' as Connor plucked the strings softly, his voice hitting the higher notes.

He put the guitar down and there was silence as he gazed across at me. I realised that he was upset as he leant back in the chair, watching me. I noticed a shell on the mantelpiece, the rough edges and grooves along the surface. It had a rainbow pattern like mother-of-pearl.

'Where did you get the shell from?'

'Liam gave it to me,' he said.

I sensed that feeling again that he was holding back, a feeling of distrust. He was wearing a strange combination of clothes. His face was flushed from the beer as he took a swig. There was a wine glass on the table and an ashtray piled high with cigarettes. It reminded me of the time I used to find evidence of other women.

I glanced at the wine glass, remembering the tattoo parlour where he and Greg used to work. There were rows of designs on the wall, illustrations of roses, butterflies, skulls, dragons. I'd never had a tattoo, a reaction against my father. Connor had described the burning or scratching sensation of the needle as similar to being scratched by a cat.

'There were these guys down at the Emporium,' I said, remembering the one with the tattoos. 'One of them said he'd been in jail for eighteen years.'

'Probably friends of the Lonegans. I heard they had some guys out there.'

He was looking away from me and I was conscious of that sense of resentment again.

'Who are the friends you said you were going to see in the mountains?'

'They're not people you know. You remember Billy? They're friends of his.'

He stood up and I felt irritated with him.

He seemed nervous as he walked towards the doorway. 'I guess I'd better go,' he said. 'They're waiting for me.'

I walked with him to the car, where he bent forward and kissed me very lightly on the cheek. Climbing into the car, I was conscious that there was something going on.

When I glanced into the rear-view mirror, Connor was in the distance, standing near the fence, gazing towards me. He turned and disappeared towards the building.

I drove back along the highway, thinking about an incident when Connor hadn't supported me, a bullying incident at work. I was right to break up with him, I told myself. He'd been mixing with a group of people before I'd left who were similar to the types of people Liam and I had grown up with. In some ways he hadn't really broken away from them.

Turning off the highway, I drove along a dirt road. I had a compulsion to see Liam's house and drove until I reached the turn-off. Further into the forest, I could see it up ahead, nestled amongst trees that menaced like sentinels, the shape of a mountain in the distance. I pulled over and climbed out of the car, staring at fallen timber, blackened beams and scattered debris. Willing myself forward, I walked towards the house. Through the gaps in the timber, I could see glimpses of light and the shapes of trees further out. I gazed up at dark holes, conscious of smoke that still seemed to linger in the air, the shafts of charred wood pointing upwards like broken spears. The doorway was blackened and I climbed through, past the remains of a fireplace with a mirror, the shininess of the glass streaked with black. Timber leant precariously, shards of wall and planks scattered on the floor, a thick coating of grey and white ash. The floor of the kitchen had almost collapsed and I made my way around the shattered floorboards.

Liam's room was at the back and I felt ill as I stood there, not wanting to go further. I was conscious of silence as I edged up against the wall and stood at the entrance to his room. It was severely burnt, the remains of furniture, the bed a twisted metallic steel frame, tufts of kapok curled around coiled springs. There was a vertical ripple down a dresser where the intense heat had seared the wood. The wall was like a blotchy wash of grey watercolour, a thick pattern of grey ash, pieces of wood and board on the floor.

I stood there for a moment, feeling nauseous, staring down at a burnt-out shell beneath the floor, conscious of a sickening silence. Through the damaged beams I could see the foundations of the house, the blackness of the earth beneath. It was where Liam's body had been found, burnt beyond recognition. I studied the earth, feeling sick, and backed out of the house.

I thought I saw something in the bushes as I climbed back into the car, but it was only a bird flying towards the branches, its wide wings black against the sky. Radic's house was supposed to be on the other side and I continued deeper into the valley, passing by rocks. The road descended towards the river shrouded in the pearly and luminescent light of a mist.

There was a fork in the road, the left leading on towards the gorge. I slowed the car slightly, then continued towards the bottom of the slope. A house was up ahead through the trees as I made a sharp descent away from the ridge.

I could see an old wooden structure in the distance, the thundering sound of water audible as I opened the window, a fresh sensation in the air, away from that smell of smoke around Liam's place. The house was shaped like a chalet with a steep triangular roof. A misty light shone through the spindly bent trunks of trees.

A man was chopping wood in a clearing, his back to me. When he turned slightly, I could see that he was dark with an angular face. I looked closely to see if he was the man I'd seen in the forest but he looked different. He was wielding the axe, sharp blows, and my nervousness increased as I heard the blade thwacking into the wood.

A boy, thin and wearing baggy jeans, was standing nearby. He studied me suspiciously as I slowed the car. I recognised him as the son of Freya and Tyler's neighbours. I had that same feeling that I'd had on the beach, a sense that someone else was watching me from the house, even though the man and boy were immediately in front of me.

Climbing out of the car, I wondered if the man was Radic. He moved away from the wood. A white dog ran towards the car, but the man called out to it and it backed away towards him, barking and running up.

'I was looking for Radic.'

He studied me and nodded towards the house. I watched as he stepped back, aiming the axe towards a large chunk of wood. The boy was still watching me and he looked away quickly.

Nobody came when I knocked on the door but I noticed someone through the glass. When the door opened, a man stood before me. He looked similar to the man I'd seen on the porch at Freya and Tyler's. His face was angular with sharp features, similar to the boy's. For a moment he seemed hostile. He stood there, towering over me, his spare frame reminding me a little of my father's.

The boy had come up onto the steps and looked away awkwardly when he saw me glance back at him. 'We thought it was Tyler and Freya,' he said, as if he were somehow responsible for my presence there. 'It's their car.'

'I was just driving by Liam's place,' I said, aware that the other man was studying me from the woodpile. 'I'm Sarah, his sister.'

I noticed the boy look away again but he gave me a surreptitious glance. He backed away down the steps as if cowed by the man's presence.

'Come in. I'm Radic. Liam left something here.'

I wondered what Liam had left behind as I followed him inside. Radic was silent as he led me into a room with two couches, made of dark brown leather, old mottled wallpaper on the wall, a murky grey colour above wooden panelling.

He sat down and stretched out his long lanky legs. 'I suppose you know about my daughter?' He said it in a serious tone as he gestured to me to sit down.

I wasn't certain what to say and stared back at him for a moment. He looked similar to Dan, Freya and Tyler's neighbour, but his face was more angular and he was taller and thinner.

'I'm sorry, I don't know much about it.'

I remembered the black dog that had run at me when I was backing out of the garage and the image of an animal in the bush when I'd been talking to Freya. Freya had said Radic's dogs came close to their house. I watched him as he settled back into the couch.

'I was away, otherwise I would have come to Liam's funeral. We would have met then.'

I heard something scratching near the door and, glancing around, noticed the shadow of a cat pass by.

'I wanted to ask you, I don't know if Jet's been causing any trouble. I ran into someone when I was out walking. The man seemed quite angry at him. I thought he might be someone who lives around here.'

Radic moved his legs a little. 'There's no one out here, except me. Jet often comes here. Liam and Lola used to take him on walks.'

He stared at me and I shifted my position on the couch, not wanting him to vent his anger at Freya and Tyler on me. I remembered Freya's comments that the family were 'good haters' and, beginning to feel stressed, I glanced anxiously at the door.

He reached over for a packet of cigarettes, pulling one out of the packet, offering me one. I shook my head.

'I think Zac knows where Lola is,' he said, lighting the cigarette. 'He says he doesn't but I think he does. Him and Tyler.' There was a hostile tone in his voice.

I was distracted by a guitar in the corner and wondered when he was going to give me the thing that Liam had left here. I studied him as he reached for the ashtray. He had a penetrating look and I sensed he was smarter than he appeared.

'I suppose you know about it all. Liam said you had your problems with Tyler.'

I frowned at him, glancing back at the guitar in the corner. It looked similar to one my mother had owned, a similar age, and I remembered the music I'd heard coming from the neighbours' house. I was preoccupied with the guitar and wasn't really concentrating.

'Nobody really knows what happened with Tyler's mother,' Radic said. 'Her suicide seemed staged.'

I tried to take in what he'd said. 'Freya said Tyler didn't like speaking about his childhood. I had to respect it in the end. They're both very private.'

He looked sceptical and I glanced over towards the guitar again.

'The thing Liam left here, he was going to give it to you. He gave it to Lola.'

There was a thin smile on his face and I noticed a vague resemblance to Ava, Lola's sister, the girl at Liam's funeral. I wondered if he was going to give me the guitar but he stood up and walked to a box on the mantelpiece, pulling out an amulet on a leather cord. It was a silver spider.

'Here,' he said.

It looked like some cheap thing that my mother had bought at the markets. I wondered why Liam had left it here. I took it from him, disappointed that it wasn't the guitar.

Radic had a faint smile on his lips, almost a little sardonic.

I glanced at the guitar again and wondered for a second if the necklace truly belonged to my mother. Liam had said the neighbours were cunning.

There was an awkward silence. He seemed to be enjoying my discomfort as if it were some kind of test.

'So you don't know anything about Tyler?'

I shook my head. 'No, not really.'

'Well, there's been rumours. Not many people know about it. It was all hushed up, his mother's suicide. People have started talking about it, up the coast.'

I frowned at him, conscious that he sounded angry. It made sense to me now why Lola would want to get away from him. There was something unpleasant about him.

'I don't know anything about it,' I repeated. 'Freya did say a long time ago that there'd been something but she said he didn't like talking about it. I had to leave it alone in the end.'

I realised this explained why Tyler didn't like discussing his parents, his issues with women. I glanced around the room. One wall was painted a brown or faded red or crimson colour with dusty, worn wallpaper. The black screen of a large TV dominated the room.

'At the beginning I liked him,' Radic said. He was scrutinising me now. 'But then there was something about him, something not right. People think his mother's death was set up, made to look like a suicide.'

It was as if he were parodying the gossip, saying the worst things he could think of. He shifted his position on the couch, staring back at me, and I had that feeling again he was playing with me, watching my reactions. There was a smell of furniture polish coming from somewhere down the hall.

When I turned back, outside, through the window, I could see the white dog.

'So you think it was actually a homicide?'

He shifted back against the couch. 'That's what people are saying. There were rumours about it and there was no note either.'

Liam hadn't left a note. That was one of the reasons people had said it was an accident.

I noticed something cunning in his expression and glanced away from him, feeling nervous. I was conscious that he was watching my reactions in a way that made me uncomfortable.

For a moment he hesitated, then he said, 'I don't know if Lola's disappearance was connected to Tyler and his mother, if Lola found out something and Liam was wondering too. I know it was difficult for him with your father. He was a moody bugger, thought too much about things. I just get on with it. It's a shame he got so involved with Tyler. I think he disliked him in the end.'

I felt something sinking in me, an unpleasant compression in my chest and throat. 'Liam didn't tell me that there was anything wrong, although I knew he was depressed.'

'Well, you'd drifted apart, that's what he told me. He often spoke about it.'

He seemed angry like Freya and Nathan at the Emporium, almost as if he blamed me. I didn't like the way he was studying me and I looked away, trying to control my emotions. I felt that compression in my throat again, a feeling of guilt and rage.

'Do you know Jon Graham? He's organising a jam session. Jon said he knew you.'

'Yeah, I remember Jon,' I said. 'He was a friend of my father's.'

'He's a friend of Julie's too. How long has it been since your father saw Julie?'

'I don't know. Quite a while, I think.'

He began talking about the time he'd worked at a nightclub on the coast, how I should go to Jon Graham's jam session. He seemed to have changed tack, talking in a fatherly way, and he commented that Tyler used to work at the nightclub as a bouncer. 'I've met your father,' he said gruffly. 'But I only met him when I came down here, just recently in fact.'

I heard someone near the doorway and when I looked up it was Ava. She seemed surprised to see me there.

'Are you coming, Dad?' she asked.

'Yeah, just a minute, Ava.' He stood up impatiently. 'Sorry, I have to go. I'm seeing some friends.'

I walked outside with him, wondering if they were the same people Connor was seeing in the mountains. He turned to face me, studying me with narrow eyes as I looked back at the others who were near the woodpile. The man who'd been chopping wood was watching me and appeared to smile faintly. He looked familiar but I couldn't place him. I watched him talking to the boy and could see that he trusted him. He appeared to be smiling, gesturing loosely, and the boy began playing with the dog, throwing a stick to him. I glanced back at Radic, thinking he might introduce us, but he ignored them.

'Well, I might see you around,' he said.

I drove off, wondering if he was manipulating me and whether he was exaggerating about Tyler's mother, deliberately stirring up trouble, or if it was something more sinister.

Turning onto the highway, I noticed a house on the side of a hill, remembering my feeling that Freya wasn't telling the truth. She'd mentioned something traumatic in Tyler's past, but the context at the time was more to do with his parents' relationship, like a divorce, something to do with property.

A car was pulling up outside as I arrived back and Dan, Radic's brother, climbed out. He was with his wife, who seemed to shuffle along beside him, a little like Jet. She was even bent low.

Dan's expression was taciturn as he glanced across at me. As I walked towards the door, I could see the resemblance between him and Radic. They were a different build, but there was something similar in the bone structure of the face. Glancing away, I walked inside and noticed Tyler down the hallway. He was walking towards the kitchen.

The remnants of the cobweb were still in my room as I walked inside and I studied the intricacy of the strands, pulling them away. I remembered the cobwebs in the attic with the owl as I pulled out the amulet. My mother had always been fascinated by webs, the complex interweavings and silky texture. Maybe that's why she liked the amulet. I looked at the thin silver legs of the spider, stretched out from its body like a star. They were sharp against my fingers as I held it.

There was a man outside in the yard talking to Dan and I put the amulet back in my pocket, clutching it lightly, feeling the spikes of the legs. I watched the two men leave the yard and walk up the steps. They paused for a moment, studying something at the side of the house.

I walked down to the kitchen, where Tyler was talking to Freya.

'I just saw Radic. He gave me something belonging to my mother. An amulet of a spider.' I hesitated for a moment, wondering whether to mention Radic's comments about Tyler's mother, or if it would be better to speak to Freya alone.

Tyler was standing close to me and I glanced across at Freya, who looked at me expectantly.

'I've never seen the amulet before,' I said. 'There was a guitar there like one my mother had. When he said he was going to give me something, I thought it would be the guitar but it was the amulet.'

'It probably was your mother's guitar. Liam said he left it there. He was teaching Lola to play it.' Freya looked at me as if I were foolish, a slight hint of contempt in her eyes.

I remembered my feeling that Radic was manipulating me. There were his sardonic looks, an apparent confidentiality, and there was that feeling of disconnection that was similar to the one I'd had on the beach. It reminded me of people my parents knew, the constant intrigue and betrayal.

'I told you to stay away from him,' Tyler said angrily. 'He was testing to see if you said anything useful about us.' He was gazing at me coldly now.

I wasn't sure whether to believe him and felt confused by Radic's odd behaviour.

Tyler clicked his tongue impatiently and walked out onto the porch. He looked furious. I glanced back at Freya and noticed a strange shift in her eyes.

'What did Radic say to you?'

'Just about his mother. He told me about her suicide.'

Freya glanced outside. Tyler was in the yard. He still looked angry. Freya walked into the laundry, lifting some washing, damp and heavy, from the machine. I followed her out to the line.

'He never wanted me to talk about it,' she said, turning to face me. 'That's why I've never mentioned it, but people have been spreading rumours. It's only just started to happen, mainly up the coast, innuendo at first, but now it's getting worse. His mother killed herself after she was involved with a younger man. Tyler was sixteen when it happened.' She began hanging out the washing.

Tyler was over in the corner near the fence. He looked agitated as he climbed over the fence and walked towards the neighbours'. I wondered if he was going to confront them about Radic and remembered the amulet as I studied the branches that stretched up towards the sky. It must have been something my mother bought after Liam and I had left, when we'd stayed with our grandparents. We'd spent some time with them when our parents were trying to work out their problems. Maybe it was some kind of talisman, something to keep her safe. I listened to the whipping and full-throated sound of a bird. It was the season of magpies, swooping down.

'Don't say anything to him about his mother,' said Freya. 'I knew it was going to come out but it will just make things worse. There's a few things I was going to tell you. What was it you said once? "Anyone who thinks he's perfect is either a fool or a liar."'

It was unlike Freya to be philosophical and I wondered what she was getting at.

'I've decided to keep an open mind about Darcy,' she said, glancing back at me. 'I don't know what she's up to. She knows some of the people on the coast. I want to find out about it. That's why I want her down, not because I'm interested in her.'

I watched her clutch a blouse and pin it carefully to the line. I could see how tense she was, the rigid grip of her fingers when she turned back to the line and resumed her pegging.

'I got the impression from Liam once that Tyler's father was the controlling type.'

'Yes, that's true. He was controlling but even so, they were close. It was traumatic for Tyler when his mother died. He's never liked talking about it. He made me promise not to say anything. I think she messed the guy around.'

She turned away from me and I remembered the child who'd died. That was probably what she was alluding to before when she said there were a few things she was going to tell me.

'Ivy said something to me about an accident when you were a child.'

Freya reached up to the line again and I watched her closely to see how she reacted.

She looked strangely detached. 'I have no memory of it,' she said.

'What do you mean? None at all?'

'Well, hardly anything. I was very young and I think Darcy exaggerated it. I mean, it was an accident.'

I glanced across at the neighbours' yard, concerned that she seemed evasive. Tyler had disappeared. A girl walked out of the house next door and sat down on the couch on the porch. She had a pale face, long dark hair.

Freya glanced up for a moment and flinched when she saw her. 'It's Celeste, a friend of theirs. She knows Aden too.'

The steps to the veranda were broken. Jet was nosing around the side of the house. He walked up the steps and the girl bent down and patted him. She was staring at us in a way that made me uncomfortable and I looked away. She seemed to be squinting at us.

'I don't like the way she's looking at us.'

'Just ignore her,' said Freya. 'They do it deliberately.' She finished pegging the clothes on the line and was looking away from me towards the trees.

I watched as the girl shot me a curious look. She'd come down to the yard and was playing with the horse's reins, patting it, smoothing her hand over its flank. I was conscious she was watching me when she thought I wasn't looking as Freya walked back inside. I walked over to the fence. She was still studying me, pulling back a little, fiddling with the reins. I glanced around to see if Jet was about. He was standing near the horse. She began playing with him and I had a feeling she was doing it deliberately. She left the horse and when she came closer she looked directly at me. Her face was thin and pale but as she paused by the fence, I noticed scabs on her arms. She pulled her shirt down when she saw me staring at them. I glanced down at her hands, which were small and knotted, and I noticed the thin ragged outline of her shoulders.

'Hi.' Her voice was high-pitched, sing song, like a child's. She bent down and picked up a stick, making a scratching sound on the fence with it.

I couldn't help smiling, thinking about her name, because she didn't look celestial.

'I don't like him much,' she said, gesturing towards Freya and

Tyler's place. She bent down towards Jet. 'I was friends with them for a while and also your brother. He was good to Lola. I liked him but I had an argument with them. Tyler told me to get off their land. It was when they lived in the mountains and now people are suspicious of them because of Lola.'

'Hasn't Radic been to the police about Lola?'

'Yeah, but she's left before. They don't take any notice of him. I suppose some people don't want to be found. That's if she's still alive.'

'Why wouldn't she want to be found?' I felt that constriction in my chest again, thinking of Liam as I watched her playing with a stick.

'Maybe she doesn't want to be found,' she repeated. 'That's what I think. Or maybe Tyler's done something to her. He didn't like her relationship with Zac. Maybe that's what's happened. They were very close and Tyler didn't like it.'

I frowned at her and glanced back at Freya and Tyler's place. Celeste turned towards the bush and walked away.

The trunks of trees emerged from the forest, leaning precariously towards the path, a mass of leaves and a pale green light. I walked back to the house, watching Celeste as she moved quickly towards the neighbours' place.

Tyler was in the kitchen. He looked angry, probably still brooding about me seeing Radic.

'I just saw this girl next door, Celeste. She was worried about Lola.'

He moved to the window, studying the garden. When I turned back, he looked at me quizzically.

'She's a fool,' he said angrily. 'I wouldn't take any notice of her. She's a friend of Aden's. The neighbours didn't know who the man in the forest was, by the way. The guy you saw with the dog, the one who doesn't like us.'

I felt uncomfortable, the intensity of his gaze. 'Radic didn't seem to know either.'

'So you spoke to him about it.'

'Yeah, he didn't know.'

I thought about Celeste's comments, how she didn't like Tyler.

He sighed, glancing back towards the bush. 'I'm thinking of leaving completely, so we'll rent in the mountains. It's near the waterfall and the area where that bushranger used to live, with the rocks and caves. There's a legend that it was inhabited by ghosts. I don't want to be beaten. I don't want to be driven away.'

'Don't the Lonegans live near there?'

'No, they've moved. It's not near them any more.' He picked up Jet's ball and bounced it like Freya had done earlier. 'We might visit Zac when we take Darcy up the coast tomorrow. He's nearby. I'll be interested what you think of Darcy. You're smart. I don't think she has Freya's interests at heart.' He walked back to the window and stared out at the yard.

Jet had strayed into the garden amongst the plants. Tyler came back and sat down at the table, leaning forward. I watched him and felt a little sorry for him. He looked so exhausted.

'Yeah, it'll be good when we move,' he said. He appeared distracted as he glanced towards the window again. 'Nothing can ever be proved about what Radic does, you know. He's very smart, cleverer than people think.' He'd always had a blind spot about admitting he was wrong and I wondered if Radic was similar, if they were locked in an egotistical battle. Maybe they'd simply aggravated each other, a personality clash.

He left the table and walked to the window, standing there for a moment as if he wished he wasn't here.

I moved over and watched him as Freya walked in. She began making dinner and glanced across at me as I helped her place the cutlery down on the table.

'Remember when Darcy was last down here?' said Tyler, sounding agitated. He reached over for the bread and seemed irritated when Freya didn't respond. 'She was provoking me.'

Freya turned away, ignoring him.

He got up and walked to the fridge, bringing some wine over. 'Honestly, there's no point resolving things. She's the sort of person you can never resolve things with and she's stirring up trouble. You know she knows Radic, probably Aden too.'

He sounded drunk and I wondered if he'd been drinking with the neighbours. Freya looked moody as Tyler offered me some wine and I noticed his hands, calloused and large, as he picked up his glass. Freya served some dip and crackers and Tyler took a hunk of bread, dipping it in the guacamole. I wondered what Darcy had been saying about him.

'What happened to the bread, Freya? It's stale. It would have been nice to have fresh bread. This is the loaf from yesterday.'

I could sense the tension in him as she brought some more bread and fruit to the table. He began peeling a peach. He offered Freya some and she shook her head.

'Are you going to see your father, Sarah?'

'Yeah, I want to ask him about Liam, about this guy he saw.'

Tyler stared at me. I wondered what he was thinking as Freya walked to the oven. She looked unhappy and I helped her with the food as we served dinner. Tyler took a few mouthfuls, Moroccan chicken and couscous. He pushed it away as if it tasted bad and reached over and dipped some more bread in the guacamole.

'I don't know why you invited Darcy, Freya. I mean, what's the point, really? Alison's your real mother. It's the same with the scattering of Scarlett's ashes. You didn't really consult me about her coming. She could have come at a better time. Sarah's here for a start. There's something sly about her and the way she blamed you for that little girl's death. How could she do that?'

'We did talk about her coming down but she only just rang,' said Freya. 'She said she'd seen my stepfather and wanted to talk about it.'

'She could have talked to you on the phone.'

'You're overreacting. You can't talk on the phone about important things. I want to find out myself what's happening with her.'

I realised now that she probably wanted me here to act as a buffer between Tyler and Darcy. No doubt, she'd been planning it all along, having Darcy down here and me keeping things in check so it didn't turn into a bloodbath. She looked distracted as she passed me some salad. I felt irritated with her, the way she seemed to be locked in her own drama and people were merely players in it. She'd obviously planned to tell me everything eventually about the child's death and Tyler's mother too.

They began arguing about Darcy and I walked down to my bedroom, deciding to ring my father. I wanted to know about this man Liam had seen. I expected to see the perfume bottle but there was an empty space on the dresser and I sat down on the bed, staring at my phone. It had been a long time since I'd last spoken to my father and I braced myself as I punched in the numbers, deciding my only purpose in ringing was to find out more about Liam. The dial tone was deafening and I felt sick as I waited.

At last he responded, a faint drawl. 'Yeah, Dane here.'

There was a pause. He always did that, paused with a silence so that you didn't know if he'd walked away or didn't want to talk to you. I could hear him breathing heavily on the other end.

'It's Sarah,' I said. I didn't say anything more, conscious I was mirroring his confusion, responding in kind. 'I know it's been a long time,' I said at last. 'But I wanted to ask you about Liam.'

'I can't talk about it on the phone. You'll have to come down. Come tomorrow afternoon. I'll be here.'

I could tell this was a deliberate piece of manipulation to get me down there but I told him I'd come and hung up. He could be charming and charismatic when he was young but then his own childhood grievances seemed to catch up with him. I walked back to the kitchen, wondering what he was going to tell me.

Freya and Tyler were in the living room. I watched TV with them for a while but it was hard to concentrate. Around eleven, I went to bed, still thinking about my father, how he could be kind, then turn on you in an instant.

I drifted off to sleep, nightmares about a child falling, and when I awoke, I remembered my visit to Liam's, that dark hole burnt out in the floor near to where his bed had been. I got dressed and walked to the kitchen.

I managed to distract myself by eating a small breakfast, then I helped Freya in the garden. She mentioned that Darcy was coming around lunchtime and I told her I was going to see my father later in the afternoon. She nodded distractedly.

Around midday we were talking in the kitchen when I heard a car outside and noticed Freya tense up immediately. She walked slowly to the front of the house and I followed her, but instead of going to the door, she walked into the room opposite the study and stood at the bay window. She was waiting by the glass, staring out onto the street.

A dark blue car with tinted windows was parked outside. The door opened and a woman climbed out onto the road. She looked young, possibly early forties, and there was a fluidity to her movements as she went to the boot and pulled out a bag. Her hair was fair, and she was wearing crisp white linen slacks, her figure slim and petite. A white top flowed over the curves of her body. She looked like she worked out or did yoga and I remembered Ivy's comment that Darcy was bourgeois now and that she hadn't always been that way. I watched her pull the bag out of the boot and wheel it around the car. She moved confidently back to the boot for a moment, a little like a cat, sleek and economical with her movements. The white slacks and top complemented the tone of her hair. It was different to Freya's flaxen locks, a little darker, and I wondered if Freya's birth father was also fair.

I glanced at Freya, who was still standing tensely by the window, staring out at the road. Darcy walked back towards the car, pulling something out of the glovebox. Her movements were a little jerky now, less confident, and I wondered why Freya didn't open the door. She seemed frozen on the spot, staring out at the road, almost as if she wished Darcy would go away. Darcy walked over and adjusted the bag, dragging it along the path. She moved towards the door. I could see her clearly now, small and slim, pale skin, taut across her cheeks. She rang the doorbell and Freya breathed in deeply. I could see the tension in her as she walked to the door, back stiff, head held high.

Someone was walking down the hallway and I turned. It was Tyler.

I stood further back down the hall as Freya opened the door. Darcy's skin was pale, almost translucent, like Freya's, but it had a delicacy, not as robust as Freya's, which had a tint of olive in it. There were fragile lines on Darcy's face, suggesting that she'd spent time in the sun, which hadn't been kind to it. I studied the crisp white slacks and flowing top that seemed to engulf her small frame.

Freya kissed her, then she pulled back quickly. It was almost embarrassing. Tyler was standing further back. He looked tense and when I glanced back at him, the bulk of his body seemed to dominate the doorway. Darcy appeared to be leaning away from him. He nodded at her and she smiled formally. He began pulling the bag along the hallway, barely looking at her.

'Darcy, this is Sarah,' Freya said, turning back towards me.

There was a slight tilt to Darcy's mouth, suggesting that she hadn't expected me.

I began walking down the hall, following Freya, who was asking Darcy details about her journey. There was something rehearsed in her voice, a formality in the way she was speaking. I could hear her nervousness, while Darcy sounded composed. Tyler continued wheeling the bag towards the bedrooms. I wondered what he was thinking, as I could only see his back, but the way he was walking, the tense lines of his body, suggested he wasn't happy.

They walked into the room opposite mine and Darcy surveyed the interior. It was dark, dingier than mine, and I noticed her glance back across the hall. She had an irritated look. The room didn't have much of a view, only onto the sheds on the other side. I had the nicest guest room. She walked briskly and purposefully around the room, glancing at the interior and out into the darkness of the hall, a little bit unhappily, as if she were used to living somewhere airy and light and

Freya and Tyler's place didn't measure up. She paused by the window as Freya showed her briefly the view outside.

We walked back to the living room and I noticed her skin again, which was pale, almost ethereal. She turned to face us, delicate features, thinly drawn eyebrows. I remembered the doll and the perfume bottle, the facets of the glass, reflective and illusory. There was something brittle about her. Ivy had said Darcy didn't like other women and that Tyler thought she was weak.

Freya was standing near the window and she opened it wide to let in the air. Darcy was gazing outside. There was a stiffness in her, an awkwardness or expectation that something needed to be resolved. Tyler looked impatient and towered over Darcy as she walked past.

'Come into the kitchen and we'll have lunch,' Freya said.

We walked inside and Darcy glanced around at the furniture.

She gazed out at the veranda and garden. 'The view of the forest is beautiful, Freya. You've done so much work.' She glanced at Tyler, who didn't respond.

He walked to the fridge and pulled out some salad vegetables, helping Freya make lunch. I could see the irritation in his movements. He was barely acknowledging Darcy and seemed to gaze at her from time to time with a hint of disgust.

'Darcy, we've been thinking of going up the coast,' Tyler said.

'I haven't been there for a while. I mean, since Scarlett's memorial.'

Freya had mentioned it. It must have been a private family ceremony.

I helped Freya prepare a salad dressing. She pulled out a tablecloth, unfurling it in the air. We set the table with fancy cutlery. I sensed Freya was trying to impress Darcy, who began talking about her life in the city, an Italian restaurant near her house.

'Sarah's background is Italian.'

'Oh really?' She smiled at me with a sudden interest but there was something forced about her.

I studied her eyes, which were dark, with heavy lashes, completely different to Freya's.

'I saw Matt at a lecture in the city,' she said, turning back towards Freya.

'Don't tell me he's still giving those bullshit lectures?' Tyler said.

'They're about meditation,' Darcy replied.

Freya frowned as she ushered us to the table and Darcy sat down opposite.

'How's Zac?'

'He's fine,' Freya said.

She pursed her lips as she leant back in her chair. She seemed to be eating very little and I noticed Tyler staring at Darcy in the same way he'd watched me the previous night.

'There was a shark sighting up the coast, Darcy.'

'It wasn't in the news.'

'They don't want the publicity. It was big, a whaler or a white pointer. Maybe it's not such a good idea going up there.'

Darcy turned to Freya, who was concentrating on her meal. 'You didn't tell me you were thinking of going up the coast.'

'We only discussed it yesterday.'

'It's near to where you're moving, isn't it? That's what you said, near the mountains. I guess you know a few people there.'

'We've been talking about it,' Freya said, looking up at her.

I could see the hostility in her as she put her knife and fork down on the plate.

'I've been thinking of moving down here too.'

I saw Tyler stare at Darcy as she looked out towards the yard. He shook his head slightly.

'I've brought some things for the baby,' she said.

I remembered the doll in the bedroom, the green and white clothes and the names they'd thought of for Scarlett at first, Emmanuel and Rachel, biblical names.

'Freya doesn't know what sex the baby is,' Tyler replied.

I was conscious that he'd said 'Freya' rather than 'we' and remembered that Connor had said he didn't think Tyler had come to terms with

Scarlett's death. Darcy appeared to notice his reaction too. I could see her scrutinising him and noticed the fine lines on her face, etched slightly like a delicate parchment. There was a shrewdness in her expression as she sat back, huddled on the chair, like a tiny animal. Ivy had said Tyler thought she was weak. She didn't seem weak and there was something calculating about her. She glanced across at me and I noticed the darkness of her eyes again. I felt uncomfortable, the way she was scrutinising me, the intensity of her gaze. It was the same way she was looking at Tyler.

'How long are you staying, Sarah?'

'Oh, I don't know, a few weeks, maybe longer. My teaching contract's expired so I thought I might see if there's any work here.'

I could tell Darcy wasn't happy and remembered Tyler said she knew Radic. Tyler picked up the loaf in the centre of the table. He sliced off a piece of bread, bits crumbling away from the board. Darcy leant over and brushed them away. She did it briskly and Tyler glanced over at her, looking irritated.

'I've met your father, Sarah. He's friends with a friend of mine, Julie.'

I glanced back at her, surprised. 'Oh, you know Julie?'

There was a slight air of embarrassment, as Julie was one of my father's affairs. I could see Darcy wanted to say something, probably about my father being in jail. I wondered if she thought he was dangerous.

At last she said, 'Where does he live now?'

'Featherdale.'

She nodded, looking thoughtful. 'We only got in contact recently, Julie and I.'

Tyler mopped up some dressing on his plate with the bread. He appeared to be brooding about something. 'Is that how you know Radic?'

'Yes, through Julie.'

I could tell Freya was picking up on the tension between Darcy and Tyler.

'Darcy, would you like to see the garden between courses?' Freya asked. 'We can talk outside.'

They left the room and Tyler muttered something under his breath which I didn't hear.

He shook his head in disgust. 'I wonder what she's been saying to Radic. She was always hinting that I was somehow to blame for Scarlett's death. At first it seemed to be directed towards both of us, but then she tried to drive a wedge between us.'

I nodded sympathetically and glanced outside at Darcy and Freya who were talking in the garden. 'My father can be like that too,' I said. 'Try not to get in a bad dynamic with her.'

I stood up and walked to the window. Darcy and Freya were chatting amicably and Freya was even guiding Darcy along the garden beds.

'They look like they're getting on well,' I said, turning to Tyler. I thought I saw something shift in him, a defensiveness.

'Tell me how you go with your father,' he said. 'I'd like to know.' He moved away from me.

Freya had said that Tyler's father was controlling but he was still close to him.

Tyler walked to the sink and I stepped out onto the porch, walking down to the garden. Freya was near a bed of spinach and flowers. I told her I was going to see my father and she reached into her pocket and gave me the car keys. I went and gathered my things and walked to the garage, where I could see Freya and Darcy near the plants. They looked more relaxed with one another now and when I glanced back, Tyler was on the porch, watching them.

Tyler's sculptures were at the back of the garage and the collections of buttons were on the bench. They'd been rearranged, possibly destined for the sculptures, but it looked like he was playing some strange counting game, messing around with them, like worry beads.

I climbed into the car and backed out of the shed. To my right, I noticed something in the bushes but it was only Freya and Darcy near the path. I backed the car on to the road and began driving towards the highway, remembering the nightmares about Liam, the light of the fire, and the darkness of his body barely visible in the flames. It was true what Connor had said to me: Liam had been going downhill with depression.

There was a shark the previous summer that had attacked a young man in the waves; a shadowy white mass lurking beneath the water's surface, returning to its old hunting ground. It wasn't far from where Tyler was taking us up the coast.

The lake was up ahead, still and reflective, heavy vegetation extending back towards the mountain. Turning on the radio, I focused on the road, thinking about my father, how we'd lived in constant fear of him towards the end. Liam and I had tried to break away, not wanting to end up like him, but for Liam, it was harder. He was older, had borne the brunt of it all, my father's temper and abuse.

I continued driving, past towns and open pastureland down towards the coast. The road descended along a headland towards the ocean, which stretched out towards mountains in the north. A small huddle of shops was up ahead, seagulls fluttering near an esplanade, a young boy throwing chips. The birds squawked and scattered along the boardwalk as I drove through the town, past a building with a cream coloured facade, circular arches, painted green.

I followed the coast road, veering towards a rugged escarpment. The road dipped down to the sea. There were slabs of rock, like a platform, the water crystalline with rocks submerged beneath a greenish hue of moss. I remembered walking along it, studying a promontory in the distance.

Turning inland, I drove for some time.

My father's house appeared in the distance, a cheap duplex with a large pond in the yard, almost like a swimming pool, the water dark and murky. Wild ducks congregated along the edge or flapped amongst the reeds. I climbed out of the car, glancing down at the silt in the pond.

Walking to the door, I rang the bell and after what seemed like an eternity, my father appeared at the doorway. He stared down at me, eyes a little blank, that dead look that I'd become accustomed to, the expression I remembered from when I'd visited him in prison. I noticed that his face was now a little beaten around and sallow, his once lustrous hair wispy, eyes a washed-out blue. He moved towards me and I felt so uncomfortable I pulled back quickly, like Freya had done with Darcy. He noticed it and I felt embarrassed as I moved away from him. There was a hint of resignation in his eyes that made me feel guilty but, at the same time, I felt relieved I wasn't making physical contact.

The hallway was dark, a smell of cigarette smoke, the corridor badly ventilated. There was something distressingly awful about his circumstances and I had to remind myself about the things he'd done and that I'd found it hard to forgive him. I'd had nightmares about him pushing or hitting my mother and then her falling and cracking her skull. He insisted he'd pushed her but the prosecutor said he'd hit her. Light streamed in through a skylight in a small room to my right. There was a bedroom to my left which was surprisingly pleasant. It had a pale chenille bedspread draped over a bed with iron railings, a wooden dresser in the corner. Light shone into the room through the window. As I walked past, I wondered if he was with anyone, but it seemed unlikely.

He led me into the kitchen, which was simply furnished, a small table, a cheap lace tablecloth, and a long wooden bench like a pew. Another skylight shed light into the room. There was another room to my left, a small round table, a computer and open-backed chairs. To my surprise, there was a Hindu text on the table.

A number of pushbikes were propped up outside at the back. He closed the window in order to block out the noise that was coming from a group of people in the flat next door. The room was small and stifling.

Walking over to a bench, he began preparing coffee, turning up the

TV for a moment so that he could hear something on the news, then turning it down again.

I stared at his back. The sound of voices and the scraping of chairs drifted in through the half-open window from the duplex next door. I could hear people sitting up against the wall, ready for late afternoon drinks.

'So what happened with Liam?' I asked. I was speaking like I used to, anticipating his rages. I felt my body tense up as I studied him.

He glanced towards the window at a scraping sound outside, the people next door, shuffling around with chairs. It was as if he was primed for something. 'Yeah, there was a guy he saw.'

'What was it about?' I could hear my voice rising, that panicked sound that used to appear when I spoke to him as a child.

'Something about Tyler.' He walked over with the coffee, placing it down carefully before me.

I stared at his hands, the way they clenched the cup. They were large hands, similar to Connor's, but they were a little gnarled now from the arthritis he'd acquired from constantly playing the guitar. I remembered again what he'd done to my mother, pushed or hit her so that she'd fallen and smashed her skull.

He noticed my gaze as he sat down and leant back in his chair. He glanced away, not looking me in the eye. He often lied, large extravagant lies or general fibs to ease a difficult situation; even Connor had mentioned it.

'I don't get involved now, Sarah. Radic doesn't like Tyler. He thinks he's done something to his daughter. Liam wouldn't talk about this man, just said he saw someone who knew Tyler. I don't know anything about it.'

There was silence outside. The people next door had left and shadows had crept into the room.

He studied me as he leant back in his chair. He seemed to be staring at a point somewhere beyond me, his eyes looking a little glassy. It troubled me that he was avoiding eye contact. He had a guilty look. I recognised it from the past.

'Your brother was very headstrong. I told him not to get involved with them. The family are very difficult.'

I could see that hardness in his eyes now, the expression I'd seen when he was in prison.

Directly in front of me, to the left, there was a green painting, variegated dark blue bands against a pattern of emerald.

'What do you mean "get involved"? Freya said something about that.'

'He'd started using ice. Zac did it a bit too but I don't know if it was anything to do with that. Like I said, Radic doesn't like Tyler.'

When I glanced back, he was watching me with that guarded look. He pursed his lips, staring at me, and I thought about the few times I'd visited him in jail. I glanced sideways at his hands, conscious that I could barely look at him.

'Where did Liam get the ice?'

'From out of town, I think. I stay away from it. There are rumours that Tyler's mother took her own life. I don't know what it was about. Radic thinks it's connected to his daughter's disappearance. I think Liam tried to help her, that's what I mean by "get involved". He wanted to get her away from her family.'

He sat back in his chair, his body looser now, more relaxed. He brushed his hair back with his hand and I remembered his desire to identify with young people. The interest had always bothered me, particularly younger women.

'What do you think happened with Tyler?'

'Well, his father was supposed to be well connected, the cops, so there may have been some kind of cover-up. I don't know if Tyler was involved.' He leant back, gazing back at me with that sullen expression.

I remembered the story about his incarceration in a boys' home for theft. At the time, I wondered if such a punishment would have been meted out to a child from a well-off family. His parents had been dirt poor and his mother had actually approved of the sentence. He was a bit vague about the boys' home except to say that they were regularly ordered to strip naked and were hit, or hosed, as a form of punishment. He'd been harsh himself with physical punishment and I'd hated him for it.

I recalled the guitar at Radic's, that feeling of distrust, Radic playing with me, and I studied my father's face with its heavy lines and pale blue eyes.

He set his coffee cup down on the table and I stared back at him. I remembered him standing silently by the doorway the night the owl had flown into the room, watching and waiting as if he already knew what would unfold for us as a family, a knowingness that had bothered me. I could feel the prongs of the spider's legs against my hand in my pocket and I touched them.

My father began fiddling with a spoon, playing with it. I noticed a strange expression in his eyes, an odd emotion that I couldn't put my finger on. It seemed to be a kind of melancholy. He began talking about his life since he'd been released from jail, how he'd stopped drinking. I glanced around the room to see if I could see any evidence of alcohol, but there was nothing, no wine bottles or beer. It all looked surprisingly pristine and domestic. Then he asked me about my teaching.

'It's primary isn't it? Liam told me. You were always good with kids.'

I wondered why he'd said that when I hadn't had that much interest in kids when I was younger and he'd never had much interest in my future either. I began talking about the children I was working with, kids from migrant families who were sometimes difficult but often eager to learn.

He looked interested. 'I guess you had some of that experience when you stayed in Italy with your mother's parents.'

I nodded, irritated that he'd referred to my grandparents as 'your mother's parents', that distancing effect. I frowned back at him and remembered his changing moods, how he could be caring and then explode like a firecracker. He hesitated for a moment and I noticed the way he shifted a little in his chair, gazing back at me.

'Have you been playing the guitar?'

'Yeah,' he said. 'A bit.'

He was making eye contact more readily but I sensed him becoming distant again. I began talking about Liam but the more I spoke about him, the more uneasy he became. He was shifting away again. He kept talking about Tyler and his mother. He glanced away from me and mentioned how he'd been happier since he'd been living here. It was obvious he wasn't going to tell me anything more about Liam. He kept skirting around my questions.

It was getting late and I told him I had to go. We walked outside and I glanced back at a rose bush, thinking about my mother, how she loved rose perfume.

He looked away and I sensed something cowardly in him. A powerful anger surged in me, that sensation around the throat again, a constriction, like suffocation, and I gazed back at him, conscious that he was partly responsible for everything that had happened. He'd ground down the whole family. The anger seemed to intensify. He could sense it in me. There was a resignation in him and I turned away.

When we reached the car, he moved to the side, his hands resting on the door as he leant towards the window. 'Let me know how you're going, love.' He said it awkwardly, looking at me for confirmation that he'd said the right thing.

I didn't react and climbed in, turning on the ignition, conscious that he was still standing by the car. I nodded briefly without looking at him, then I pulled away and drove quickly, glancing back in the mirror, like I'd done the day before with Connor. He was still standing there, watching, then he turned back towards the house.

I drove on, feeling angry at myself. I wondered if I'd been too hard on him, if I should be kinder, assist with his rehabilitation, but I couldn't get past my anger. I could still see the house in the distance, in the rear-view mirror, as I reached the main road, driving on until I reached the turn-off to the mountains.

That deep sense of sadness took hold again as I thought of my mother, a feeling of grief and regret that I hadn't done enough for either her or Liam. It was a type of survivor guilt.

I continued driving, oblivious to where I was going until I realised I was close to Zac's place. There was a village up ahead, an old church, silvery grey, like the churches I'd seen in England. The mountains were in the distance, a sharp cradle of peaks.

I drove past a field, rows of lavender, and a large yew tree at the front of a fence. Dense forest covered the slopes of mountains, a blue hue on the foliage, branches reaching out like long arms or fingers. I followed a gravel path, the road stretching into the bush, a grassy strip in the centre, plants with large fanned leaves along the border of the road.

Zac's house was further along and I parked the car, staring straight ahead for a moment. Two orange brick chimneys sat on the same side of the house, a painted green picket fence, and a small porch with a veranda. Freya had mentioned on the phone that Zac was renting it from Matt. I climbed out and walked to the front door. I hadn't rung, and felt nervous as I knocked.

After a few moments, a woman appeared. She had broad cheekbones, pale skin and her eyes had pronounced circles beneath them. She stood motionless for a moment as I asked if Zac was home. She beckoned me inside. I followed her down the hallway, noticing her dishevelled appearance, long limbs, the way her shirt was hanging loose around her skirt.

'Zac,' she called out. When she reached the living room, she turned and faced me.

I felt a little uncomfortable as she scrutinised me, then we walked into the room.

I could hear footsteps down the hallway and Zac appeared in the doorway. He was more slightly built than Tyler, but appeared a little heavier than days gone by, with the same dark hair as Tyler. His face had a paler, fuller look, more cherubic and innocent, and his eyes were green like Tyler's, flecked with brown. He stood in the centre of the room, then he moved forward and kissed me.

We sat down on the couch and Zac glanced towards some bookcases in the corner. 'Sarah, have you met Brenda?'

Brenda smiled at me as she settled down on a couch opposite, pulling her legs up onto the cushion.

The room was shadowy, the couch heavy, padded with a brocade material, an ashtray on a stand in the corner. I noticed a poster of a deity on the wall, surrounded by a halo, a stained-glass pattern, a star radiating outward.

A dog wandered in and I was surprised to see it was the dog I'd noticed in the yard at Radic's, the white one. It was a cross-breed.

'Brenda, can you take the dog outside.'

Zac had a commanding tone and she stood up and walked out with the dog. I remembered Ivy saying a friend of Zac's was training Radic's dogs.

I glanced around at the bookcases and noticed that there were books similar to the ones at Freya and Tyler's, leather-bound and old.

Brenda returned and sat down on the couch next to Zac.

'You have some books like the ones back at Freya and Tyler's. Where did you get them from?'

Zac glanced towards the bookcase. 'They belong to Tyler.'

I looked towards the books, sensing he was unhappy. Some of the covers were peeling away and the spines were damaged. Zac had always called Tyler by his name rather than 'Dad', something which I'd found odd and a little precocious when he was young. It seemed to signify disrespect.

The room was slightly messy. There was a pot plant, and a pillow, back bolsters on the couch, lime green, a little old-fashioned but not intrusive. A collection of old cookbooks and games sat in a corner.

A bird squawked outside. I could see it in the trees through the window, galahs and rainbow lorikeets flying amongst the branches. Two lorikeets sat on a branch, huddled together like soldiers, perched upright and vigilant, The galah held its ground and tried to intimidate them until another galah swooped down. The lorikeets scattered, fleeing in fright.

I shifted my gaze towards Brenda, sitting opposite. Her dark hair was fluffed out around a wide-cheeked face. She was wearing a woollen hat with dangling pom-poms and pulled her long skirt tighter around her knees. My mother sometimes dressed the same way in the final years of her life. My mother's place was always cluttered too and she was a hoarder like Zac and Tyler, but for different reasons.

Zac had a more confident air than I remembered, and he had the same presence as Tyler, something imposing. I sensed that this was his domain and he was in control of it.

He smiled at me and I noticed again that he was making eye contact.

'I don't see much of Tyler nowadays,' he said. 'He didn't like my relationship with Lola.'

I nodded, conscious that a lot of the stress they were experiencing now was about him. 'I heard about some of the things that have been happening.'

He leant forward a little. 'Oh, what?'

'Just about Lola, that no one's heard from her.'

'I haven't heard from her either.'

I watched as he leant back against the couch. He was watching me and I sensed I'd given him an opportunity to air something. There was something resentful in him, as if he were sceptical about it all, and he studied me impassively.

'How are things between you and Tyler?'

'OK,' he said. 'I don't talk to him very much. Freya's birth mother's coming down. Did you know that?'

'She's here now.'

He picked up a pen from the table, twisting it in his fingers. He looked uncomfortable. 'Have you seen your father?'

'I just saw him. There was a guy who spoke to Liam, something to do with Tyler. Do you know anything about it?'

'No.'

I sensed he wasn't telling me the truth and recalled an essay he'd published on the Internet. It was an intelligently written treatise about someone who had completely changed their life. They'd had an abusive childhood, bad things had happened but they were supposed to be completely different now.

He looked at me unhappily and I wondered what he was thinking. Brenda was listening quietly, not saying anything.

Zac looked away from me towards her. 'You know, Lola's probably gone to the city. She was fed up with things, like you were when you left. I don't blame her for leaving.'

I noticed a small vase nearby. It was similar to the one back at Freya's, except that it was black. Freya had commented that Zac had changed.

'I can understand Lola leaving. I wanted a complete break too.'

I glanced over at the vase. When I looked back, Zac had a thin smile on his face. It broadened and made him look childlike. Brenda had that same searching look as she glanced up at me, the same one she'd given me in the doorway. She stood up and Zac and I were left studying each other as she left the room.

'Ivy said Freya and Liam were close.'

He looked away from me, biting his lip. 'Yeah, but it was just a friendship, though.' He shifted his gaze, studying the books. He seemed to be examining the titles, then he turned to look at me again, moving his position a little on the couch. 'So you saw your father?'

'Yeah.'

'What did he say?'

'Just about Tyler's mother, your grandmother. Radic's suspicious about Tyler. He thinks your grandmother's death is tied in with Lola's disappearance.'

I noticed his lip curl slightly and remembered his issues with Tyler.

'I don't take much notice of Radic. Lola wanted to get away from him. He can be very difficult. He's domineering like Tyler.' He looked at me awkwardly. 'Tyler never talked about my grandmother's death. I only found out about it through Aden.'

I glanced around at the worn sofa, a dirty velveteen, the large flat-screen TV, a computer in the corner and a desk piled high with notes and documents.

He was staring at me intently again. The dog had wandered back in and was sitting near a fireplace.

'I told Radic it's not right to keep dogs like that black one of his. They're wild dogs.'

'Is Jet a wild dog?'

'Yeah, partly.'

I could hear another dog barking loudly outside and I got up to look out the window. It was running back and forth across the yard.

'Who's that?' I asked, noticing a man with long fair hair.

Zac got up to have a look, leaning slightly against the windowsill. 'Josh Lonegan.'

He looked completely different, a man rather than a boy. The same transformation that was evident in Zac. I watched him walk to the side of the house, realising he was Aden's nephew as I leant against the ledge. Zac was watching him.

'I think it got too much for Liam, you know. He was like that. There was a lot of grief about your mother.' He seemed distressed.

I stepped back from the window. He must have been thinking about his own mother and I wondered if he was trying to tell me in code that foul play had happened or that Liam had committed suicide.

'It was on both sides, the rift we had. I don't know how much it got him down.'

'Yeah, he was upset about it but I never really understood what it was about.' I looked away from him, feeling guilty.

'He was a good guy, Sarah, but he could be very antagonistic. He had a temper, like your father. Maybe he aggravated someone.' Zac had an odd expression in his eyes, as if he understood more about the situation than he was saying.

I thought about Liam's temper, how he'd had problems with it, getting into fights. 'Like who?'

'Around here, it could be anyone.' He seemed to have composed himself now and left the room.

I followed him down the hallway. Brenda was in the garden. I noticed a beehive as we walked a little way towards the edge of the bush. It was a box shape with drawers and a pointed roof.

Zac glanced over at Josh, who seemed to be ignoring us, talking to Brenda. He walked amongst the nasturtiums, pulling off some parsley. I watched him eating it, breaking off pieces, crumbling them and flicking them to the ground.

Zac glanced back at me.

'I know this is hard,' I said. 'But do you think Liam might have taken his own life? It's been troubling me for a while, people's comments about the state he was in. A lot of people have hinted at it.'

He flinched. 'No, I don't think so.' His voice trailed off and he looked away, distressed.

He seemed nervous as I glanced across at Josh in the distance, talking with Brenda. I could see his fair hair, and something about his face looked familiar. He looked similar to the man chopping wood at Radic's.

I turned back to Zac. 'Is Josh related to Freya and Tyler's neighbours? I was out at Radic's yesterday and there was a man chopping wood. He looked a bit similar.'

'It was probably Tom Lonegan, his father. Josh has had a rift with his father, like I've had with Tyler.'

I followed him inside and down the corridor. There was a room to my left. The walls were a bit dowdy with paint peeling off in parts, the ceilings high and beaded, with a rose and thistle motif. The furniture inside seemed to go with the house. It wasn't exactly antique but it was old and beautiful, tables made from a dark wood like mahogany, large couches that were ancient and worn. The marble fireplace was still intact and there was an upright piano. Matt seemed to be interested in antiques. There was another room, leading off from the one I was looking at.

Zac moved forward and closed the door. 'No one's allowed inside,' he said.

'Matt seems to be an interesting guy. Freya said he was helping you.

She said you were renting this place off him.' I looked back towards the room again, conscious that Zac wanted to move further down the hall.

His hair was much shorter than I remembered. He ran his hands over his scalp grasping for the hair that was no longer there. A cigarette was burning in an ashtray on a table in the hallway, the smoke curling silently like a shadowy arabesque.

Zac bit his lip and gazed at me with a curious expression. He'd always been highly strung, that's how I'd describe him, an odd mixture of independence and vulnerability, someone who reacted like a lion cornered when things got too much for him. I sensed a secretiveness at work, continually patching up the mistakes of pride and nervous collapse.

He was fixating on me a little, smiling at me. There was an unevenness to his features and a certain hardness in his lips that lent him a generally masculine air while the pallor of his skin suggested the sickly child he'd been. I remembered his interest in Karin years ago. He was only ten years younger and had been focusing on her the last time I'd been here.

He casually brushed some ash away from the table.

'I'm worried about Freya,' I said.

There was something at work in him. He was thinking about something.

'I wouldn't worry about her. She knows how to handle herself.'

He said it in a bitter way that surprised me and I was conscious of a cynical expression in his eyes.

'Is there something wrong between the two of you?'

'No. She went through a very bad time with Scarlett, that's all.'

I paused for a moment, still conscious of his bitterness. 'We're staying at Doug's on the coast,' I said. 'Liam used to visit the Simpson place. It's part of a huge complex of buildings. I've heard about it. I thought I might go there. Liam told me he hung out there sometimes.'

'Yeah, he did. Aden lives there.' Zac paused by the doorway.

I sensed a slight air of hostility. He seemed to have clammed up.

I glanced at my watch. 'I'd better get back. I'll try and come back again when we're on the coast.'

'Yeah, if you have time,' he said.

There was a bitter tone in his voice again and when he glanced back I could see his pale eyes held back warmth. He was pulling away from me, not wanting to be touched like Tyler.

He walked with me to the car and stood back motionless for a moment as I climbed in.

I began driving back towards the highway, bothered by his manner. Zac didn't think Liam's death was a suicide but his decline seemed to date from Lola's disappearance. I felt ashamed that I'd cut myself off from him. It was possible he'd killed himself like Tyler's mother but there was no note, although he was known to be impulsive. Perhaps he'd been brooding about things. Seeing our father for the first time since he'd been released from jail might have tipped him over the edge and then there was the man he'd spoken to, someone connected with Tyler.

Liam and our father had always had an extremely volatile relationship and Liam hated him for what he'd done to our mother. I glanced up at the trees, remembering my father turning off the light to make sure the owl flew out. I'd forgotten it was there and when I'd turned the light on, the owl was staring at me. I'd screamed and it went flapping, startled, about the room. It beat helplessly against the walls, trapped and desperately trying to escape to the wild.

The old swing was in the front yard when I arrived back at Freya and Tyler's. It was twisted slightly to the right, windows looking out onto the hedge. I parked the car and walked towards the house, gazing up at the bay window that reminded me of a prism, the panes of glass angled away from each other. I could see the crack where the ball had hit the window. It was at the edge. I walked past the swing and up onto the porch. The door was ajar at the neighbours' place and I wondered if there was someone visiting them.

There didn't seem to be anyone home and I walked through to my room, where I studied the neighbours' house through the glass. Jet wasn't in the yard and I thought I saw someone closing the door that led to the porch. The trees at the edge of the bush appeared as a shadowy line in the distance. I was thinking about Connor, his strange distance and my sadness the day before, when I heard someone behind me.

It was Darcy. She had a detached expression on her face, a bit like Freya when she wasn't happy. 'I was just going outside to sit down. Do you want to come?'

We walked to the porch.

'How did you go with your father?' Her voice was low for someone so slightly built.

'OK,' I said. 'I knew it was going to be difficult.'

The white of her blouse and her creamy skin contrasted with the old wood on the porch. I saw someone closing the door on the neighbours' veranda. Darcy couldn't see them. She seemed to be studying the garden where the passionfruit vine was trailing over a fence.

'Where are the others?' I asked, watching the neighbours' yard.

'Out walking. I was wondering if you'd noticed a difference in Freya? She seems very stressed.'

She was wearing dark slacks, a black cashmere cardigan and a white blouse with an elegant grey scarf draped very loosely around her neck. It contrasted with her white skin, like the wood of the porch. I could see the delicacy of her collarbone, the slimness of her arms and the freckled tone around her neck. She took off her cardigan, her arms a little crepey, suggesting that she was older than I thought.

She made me uncomfortable and I glanced at the garden. In spite of sitting there calmly, I sensed an agitation in her, and when I glanced back, she wasn't quite meeting my gaze.

'I've been concerned about Freya for some time,' she said.

I watched as she tilted a glass on the table. It was hard to read her expression. It was perhaps one of concern or anxiety. She picked the glass up and took a sip of her drink, rotating it, so that the ice clinked against the side.

'I guess she's stressed because of the baby and Zac.'

She tilted her glass again, holding it away from her. 'Yes, that's true. Were you surprised Freya decided to stay with him, that they decided to stay here with all the problems they've had?'

I was conscious that she'd referred to Tyler as 'him'. At the same time, I was curious where this was heading. 'Yes, I was. I thought they'd leave, like I did.'

She was watching me intently now. 'I don't trust him. There's things I'm trying to find out but I can't talk about it yet. You know, I told Ray, Freya's stepfather, that Freya was expecting after losing Scarlett. I haven't seen him for a long time. We separated a while ago but I ran into him.'

I remembered the story about the child who had fallen downstairs and immediately I felt suspicious of her. Darcy sounded resentful and I didn't say anything. She swivelled the ice around in her glass and I turned back and watched as she stared out towards the bush.

'Ray's been more forgiving about it. I mean what happened with Kirrily. Freya told me she told you about it.'

'Freya was only young,' I said, feeling angry at her.

She noticed my reaction and seemed to back down a little. 'Yes, she was young when Kirrily died. I'm not surprised she doesn't remember it all. I spoke to Freya yesterday about the rumours about Tyler's mother's suicide. She doesn't want to talk about it.'

It occurred to me that Freya hadn't told me anything about the suicide because she knew I'd be onto it. She'd commented once that I was her conscience. There was always a wilful blocking out of anything difficult, a recasting of the narrative to something more palatable. I had a vague sense that she and Darcy might be on the same level, that perhaps Darcy wasn't that interested in doing anything either, and was manipulating me, that I might do something on her behalf.

'I only found out recently myself. Freya said Tyler didn't want her talking about it.'

'I'm not surprised, and you were close, but you haven't seen her for quite a while. She's lost a lot of trust in people, myself included. I did my best for her, but it wasn't easy.'

The way she was gazing straight at me now was unnerving. I felt confused, wondering what Freya had said to her.

'Tyler's stressed too, this business about Lola.'

I could tell from her expression she was expecting me to say something. 'I guess with his own childhood,' I said vaguely.

She smiled at me distantly again. I noticed that strangely stylised look in her eyes, something forced and unpleasant. A sense of jadedness took hold but I managed to refocus away from it.

'Was there domestic violence in the relationship with Tyler's parents?'

'Yes, there was,' she said. She looked at me thoughtfully now. The drink had relaxed her. 'She had an affair with a younger man and his father was very angry about it. Freya said you were close but then you left after Scarlett's death and hadn't really kept in contact. She said you were angry at her for staying with Tyler.' She had that tone in her voice again, pushing me about Tyler.

I remembered she knew Radic. Her tone was the same as Nathan's when he was talking about my leaving here after Scarlett's death, but when I studied her she was looking at me inquisitively.

I relaxed a little. 'Freya and I were close. It was difficult leaving but I was offered the teaching job. It's true I was baffled she stayed with Tyler because there was so much friction between them.'

She had a questioning look, faintly amused. It was obvious she didn't think much of Tyler and Freya's relationship. I looked across to the neighbours' garden, feeling awkward. There was a movement amongst the trees. Darcy was studying it too.

'Where's Jet?' I asked.

'With Freya and Tyler. He's a strange dog, don't you think? Not the kind I'd have. Some friend of theirs was cruel to him.'

I could hear footsteps behind me and when I glanced around Tyler was in the doorway, staring down at Darcy.

'I saw Dan from next door,' he said. 'He was complaining about Jet.'

Darcy ignored him and began talking about her work as a nurse in the city. I was surprised. I didn't see her in that kind of profession at all.

I could hear someone behind us and Freya walked out onto the porch.

'I'm making dinner,' she said. She seemed to want us inside.

Darcy stood up and I followed her in. She had a slightly guilty expression as we helped Freya prepare the meal. She was talking about the coast, how she was looking forward to it.

'We won't have time to drop in on Zac,' Freya said. 'I'm not really sure how things are going with him.'

'I saw Zac after I saw my father.'

Tyler frowned at me. 'How was he?'

'A bit moody. Josh was there.'

I could tell he was unhappy, no doubt about Zac and Josh. He seemed to sense something was wrong as he glanced at Darcy and me from time to time, frowning a little. I wanted to talk to Freya but there was no opportunity.

We watched TV after dinner and around midnight I went to bed. I was getting ready when Freya walked into the room. I looked up at her, knowing something was wrong.

'Tyler said you were talking to Darcy. I know she's been talking to Radic.'

I fiddled with my laces and pulled off my shoe.

'She mentioned Tyler's mother and the suicide.'

Freya watched me as I pushed the shoe to one side. 'It's not something Tyler likes to discuss. There were rumours that it was set up, that Tyler's father was an influential man and had a hand in it, that he knew people in the police but it's not true.' She gazed back at me.

I could see the tension in her face and was conscious that I'd had little to do with her or Liam after I'd left. I wondered if Tyler's mother's death was definitely a suicide and if Tyler's father had been involved. Who could tell with these things? My father had told me about some of the people in jail. One of them was a man who looked completely harmless but had been manipulated by other people into committing a murder. He was very vulnerable and had a bad time in jail. Other prisoners were targeting him.

'Tyler hated that she was involved with this guy but I think he felt sorry for Price in a way. That's the guy's name, Niall Price. It was humiliating for Tyler, though. He was quite young.'

She had a sad look in her eyes, something diminished, and instinctively I reached over and touched her hand. She smiled at me gratefully and shifted her position on the bed again. Then her expression became more guarded and I stared back at her, feeling troubled.

She glanced over towards the window. 'Tyler thinks it will be good to spend some time at the sea. The sea's always out of reach, don't you think? The more you chase it, the farther away it becomes. That's how I think of it, anyway, stretching out forever, but never reaching it.'

I wondered what she meant. It wasn't how I saw the sea at all. The horizon maybe, but not the sea. Then I remembered how she and Liam liked the wildness of the ocean, swimming in the waves, but the wildness conflicted with Freya's need for stability and order. I wondered if they'd been discussing it, had compared the contrasts in their personalities. I remembered the rugged cliffs further north, a wide expanse of ocean rolling towards the sand, and a heavy escarpment. It was where I thought they'd scattered Scarlett's ashes.

She lingered on the bed for a moment as I finished getting ready. I leant over to my suitcase and packed some things away. I sensed something uncertain in her, a vulnerability. When I turned back, she was studying the chest of drawers in the corner. She said goodnight and left the room and I climbed into bed.

I lay there for hours, thinking about my father and Liam, and around two a.m. I drifted off to sleep.

Around four, I awoke, studying the shadows cast by the trees.

When I awoke again in the morning, the sun was shining into the room. I looked up at the blind and the doll on the chair, conscious of someone outside, opening the door to the room opposite. I got up and had a look. It was Darcy, walking down the hallway, dressed smartly in a knitted top and slacks. I got ready and left the room, thinking about Tyler's comments about Darcy, how he didn't like her.

When I walked into the kitchen, Darcy was at the table. She was studying Tyler, looking a little judgemental.

'Are you going to take some of your art material with you, Tyler? Have you had any success with it?'

Her voice had a sarcastic tone and I looked at her nervously.

'Yeah, I will,' he said. 'Although there's some stuff up at Billy's cabin. It's near Doug's place.'

'Yes, I've heard of Billy. Julie told me about him.'

I thought of the buttons and sculptures in the shed.

Darcy got up and walked outside. Tyler watched her as she stood on the porch, holding her coffee. There was a coldness in his gaze. She walked slowly to the edge, staring out at the bush, and I noticed Tyler frowning slightly.

'How come there's only two houses here?' I asked. 'You and the neighbours. It's so isolated but they're close together.'

'They were both owned by the same family,' Freya replied. 'The grandparents lived in one and the kids and grandchildren in the other. They liked the remote location and the land was in the family for a while.'

I could see the tension in Tyler's back and the bulk of his body as he stood up and walked to the bench. He was watching Darcy outside. His jumper dipped around his neck, the area where Freya had patched it.

'I want to stop at the marina,' he said. 'Check what Doug's doing. I think I'll take Jet with us.'

'Are you going fishing with Doug?'

'Yeah, he offered to mind Jet. We can use the dinghy if you don't want to come out with us on the cruiser, Sarah.'

'I just wasn't feeling well that day I went out with you and Doug.' I helped Freya collect some plates, remembering how sick I'd become on Doug's boat, the choppy waves. I'd been unable to keep my balance.

Freya glanced out at Darcy, who was still on the porch. She was pressing up against the railing.

'Do you think everything will be all right with her?' I asked as Tyler left the room.

'I hope so,' said Freya in a low voice. 'Tyler promised he'd make more of an effort. She might leave early, anyway. I think she came to convince me to leave Tyler. We argued about it yesterday. I think she might stay with Julie.'

Darcy moved closer to the edge of the porch and didn't turn round. There was music coming from the neighbours. I watched her turn and glance at Jet, who had shifted a little on the porch, wandering up to her. She moved away from him. I could see the agitation in her movements.

No one was in the neighbours' yard when I left the kitchen and went to my room. I could hear clatter outside, someone walking down the hallway as I packed my bag. I sat down on my bed for a moment, thinking about Freya. There was an anxiety in her as if she were building up to something, summoning strength.

The others were waiting for me when I walked outside, and Tyler had an expectant look as we left the house. Darcy looked away from me. She walked a little ahead, slowly at first, glancing back at Tyler, who was to my right. He seemed to be cut off as usual as he looked around for Jet. I remembered the things Darcy had said the night before and glanced across at Freya but she didn't meet my gaze. She seemed distracted as we climbed into the car.

Tyler turned on the engine and we drove along the dirt road towards the highway. I studied the black image of the road as it unfurled towards the mountains and the coast.

Darcy wasn't saying anything, just listening to the music on the radio. From time to time, she glanced at Freya and Tyler, who were speaking about someone on the coast.

'Well, what do you expect?' Tyler was saying. 'I don't really know what he was up to. Meddling as usual. Do you think I should have it out with him?'

Jet was next to Freya and Tyler. Darcy looked a little melancholy, that same expression I'd observed with Freya when she was contemplating something. Jet was shuffling around a bit and Freya reached out and touched him. He seemed to relax onto the seat away from her.

Tyler fiddled with the volume on the radio and I noticed his shoulders hunch, the tension in his neck. The highway stretched ahead of us, two white lines in the centre creating a wavering mirage, the descent of a cliff on my right. There was grass dotted with white flowers and down below, the lines of waves lapped towards a pale rim of sand.

I began thinking about Zac. There was something troubling me about him and Freya too.

A row of shops came into view and a cluster of boats around the bay further along, not far from where we were heading. It occurred to me that this might be where Tyler wanted to go fishing in the dinghy if we didn't go out on Doug's cruiser. I sensed he wanted to be alone, that he wanted to think about things and it wouldn't surprise me if Freya, Darcy and I were left alone at the house.

Darcy wasn't saying anything. She looked anxious as we approached the marina and Tyler parked the car outside. We climbed out and Darcy walked a little ahead of us.

Doug was standing at the counter when we walked inside. He stared at Darcy as if he wasn't surprised to see her there. There was something different about him. He seemed more wary and reserved. He was wearing a T-shirt that looked grimy as if he'd been working out on the boats and seemed to be assessing Darcy. 'Tyler, everything's ready for you up there. You can come with us out on the boat if you want.'

'As long as it's not too rough. Sarah gets seasick. Remember?'

'We can take you out. I'm more experienced than Tyler.' He made a joke about Tyler's navigation skills.

I glanced through the doorway at a woman sunbaking outside on a deck.

Doug saw me looking at her. 'That's my niece. She might come out with us.'

'Your niece?' Tyler said in a slight mocking tone.

'Yeah, you know, Linda's daughter.'

'I'll let you know when I'll be in town. I have to see a few people, so I'll come down later.'

Doug was still staring at Darcy. She was walking back along the wharf, looking down at something in the water. Freya followed her.

Tyler had that cold expression on his face and Doug didn't say anything. He glanced at Tyler, then he began talking about fishing further north. 'Graeme caught a marlin, did you know that?'

I walked over to some maps in the corner as Tyler went with Doug back along the wharf towards the cruiser. I could see them talking through the window.

A man came into the shop. He looked familiar, red hair, slim build. Feeling uneasy with the way he was staring at me, I walked outside and caught up to Freya and Darcy. They were walking ahead to the car. Tyler was still talking to Doug at the other end.

I heard footsteps and when I turned it was Tyler. He walked towards the car and we climbed inside. He was scowling in the mirror and he turned to look at Freya as if he were uncertain what to do.

'You know, you should mind your own business, Darcy. It's the same thing as last time. You know nothing about what happened.'

There was silence for a moment. Doug must have said something to him about Darcy spreading rumours about his mother's death. She bit her lip and I listened to white noise from the radio, an intense crackling sound as Tyler fiddled with the dial. He leant forward, gripping the wheel and began driving along the road.

We drove for some time, listening to the music, and Tyler turned down the volume.

'The house is just over the rise. There's quite a bit of bush behind it that goes inland towards the mountains.'

Freya's shoulders tensed as we took a detour and swerved around a bend. Tyler was driving aggressively. I saw a house in the distance on top of a cliff that led away towards the ocean. There was a clear area behind it and then dense bush that led further back. The house was perched precariously and looked a little like a flying saucer. The windows had a conical shape, wide glass looking down onto the water. The beach led to a headland in the distance which is where I thought they'd scattered Scarlett's ashes. I glanced at Darcy, remembering that she'd been at the memorial gathering. Directly below the house there were rocks.

Tyler parked the car and I had a bracing sense of the sea air as we climbed out and walked towards the door. I'd walked on the headland further north with Connor, passing by a tree not far from the area where they'd scattered Scarlett's ashes.

I wondered what Tyler was thinking. He seemed moody and looked back at Darcy as if he wished she wasn't there. We climbed the remaining section of the driveway. Darcy was silent as Tyler fiddled with the key. I could sense the tension between them as he shuffled the different keys around on the ring until he found the right one. I studied them in the sunlight, blinking a little as I stared up at the balcony on the house next door.

Tyler opened the door and we walked into a large living room with a fireplace. Darcy surveyed the room, like she'd done back at Freya and Tyler's. She seemed more at ease now and Freya stood by the fireplace watching her. Blocks of wood had been stacked nearby, a fireguard with a pattern like a four-leaf clover, ornate, a bit like Zac's vase. Drapes hung by the side of the window. Against the wall there was a dark leather lounge suite and an enormous television and stereo system in the corner. It looked expensive and I wondered how Doug could afford it. Then I remembered Tyler had said he'd had a windfall with tourists in the last season, taking them out on cruises, so perhaps that was it.

Tyler showed me my room, which was at the back of the house, with a large window looking out onto the garden. I began unpacking my things. I could hear Tyler and Darcy arguing and was seized with an intense need to rid myself of everything that had been going on, memories of my father and his violence, Liam, and all the discussion about Tyler and his mother.

I collected my swimming things. 'I'm going to the beach,' I said, walking out to the living room.

Freya was lying on the couch, looking tired. 'I'll rest for a bit,' she said. 'I'll make lunch when you're back. Maybe a barbecue. We might go fishing later, take the dinghy out, although Doug said there's some fish in the fridge.'

Darcy was by the fireplace. I could tell she knew I wanted to be alone and she smiled at me faintly as I left the room.

When I walked outside, I glanced back and noticed a small figure standing at the window looking down towards the sea, pressed up against the glass. It made me uneasy, the faint shape of the figure against the glass. I dismissed the feeling as I walked down the driveway.

Glancing back, I noticed another house nearby. It was supported by white poles, the upper level a darker brick, black windows set back against dense greenery. I thought I saw someone standing on the balcony, dressed in jeans and shirt gesticulating towards the ocean. They seemed to be talking on a phone.

Waves broke onto the shore as I climbed down the path towards the beach. I began thinking about the antagonism between Darcy and Tyler, wondering if it had a bearing on his mother. It reminded me of my parents, how Liam always seemed to come between them, trying to break it up.

There had been a time when our dog had leapt up and attacked our father, trying to protect me, and he'd lashed out, injuring it with a knife. The dog was in shock, just as Moon had been when he was hit by the car, silent, but looking at me stoically, with that dumb acceptance that I was going to do something. My father had dropped the knife and I'd seen him trembling. I'd felt sickened by his hypocrisy when he'd returned from the vet acting as if the dog had been injured in a car accident.

There was an odd whistling noise like the melancholy siren of the sea as I walked down to the beach, glancing down at a shell on the sand. I remembered the mother-of-pearl shell I'd found, the sound of the waves thundering onto the shore. The shell had been wedged within the sand, a delicate lip, and I'd plucked it out. My parents had been sitting some distance away, bending towards one another, and there had been an air of tension between them. It was the day after my father had injured the dog. I'd picked up the shell and examined the rough edges and grooves along the surface. It had a rainbow pattern. The surf had swirled around the rock at the base of the cliff and I'd run away from them towards the end of the beach. My father had always told me to stay away from the cliffs as there were dangerous rips but I'd wanted to feel the sensation of the water swishing around me, pulling me out to sea, so I'd plunged into the ocean, swimming out until I'd reached the waves.

There was a long stretch of sand unfurling towards the headland now and the wind blew sand towards me, hitting my legs. I noticed mounds of foam at the water's edge and remembered the clusters of foam on the beach as a child, how Liam and I used to sit in it, touching the bubbles, bursting them and watching them break or drift away. I bent down, picking up some driftwood, similar to Tyler's sculpture back at the house, examining it, then leaving it on the sand.

There was a woman further along. She ran towards the water and dipped below the waves. The beach stretched away into the distance as I listened to the rhythm of the waves, rolling towards the shore. When I glanced back, I thought I saw someone further along. It looked like a young man. I could just make out a figure, small and slim. He seemed to be running towards me. I strained to see who it was, but it was difficult to tell. He was running swiftly but then he doubled back, running away from me.

Trees twisted away from the cliff in the distance and I could see the other cliff, the one where they'd scattered Scarlett's ashes. It jutted out towards the ocean and had a sharp drop.

Seagulls clustered on rocky outcrops towards the south, the swell of the breaking waves swirling around my ankles. I stood there, watching the water swish around my feet. Then I dived beneath the waves. A surge of current dragged me under through a funnel of water and I remembered the shark that had attacked a young man the previous season, as the surf pushed and twisted my body. Fighting my way upward, I gasped for breath, the whoosh of the waves thundering against my ears, the currents pulling me back.

Panicking, I swam towards the shore, and noticed a pale light further along. It looked like a campfire, a distant glow, and I remembered a man walking towards me, the day before Liam died, his face obscured by the board brim of a hat.

I walked back across the sand and climbed the hill to the house, trying to get the image of Liam burning out of my mind, an horrific sight, skin melting over his face.

Windows loomed down from the house above as I climbed the driveway, a ray of sun shining through the parting clouds onto the plants in the garden, creating crescents on the warm soil beneath the leaves. I opened the door and glanced up at the glass in the stairwell, kaleidoscopic images, like flashes of fairy lights in a tree, a light shining down on me. I could hear Tyler talking to someone inside. I paused for a moment, not sure who he was talking to.

'Yeah, you're right, but what can I do?'

When I walked inside, a man was standing near the couch. He was wearing a leather jacket and dark slacks.

Tyler flinched when he saw me. 'Sarah, this is Matt.'

So this was the psychologist Zac and Freya liked. He looked urbane, hair neatly cut in a fashionable way, curly around the temples. His clothes were expensive, an overall appearance that seemed more in place in the city. He must be well off, the way he was dressed, the house that Zac lived in with the antiques. He smiled at me and it seemed strange that Tyler was talking to him in an amicable fashion when there'd been animosity between them. Some kind of male solidarity had trumped an underlying hostility but then I noticed that Matt was standing a little tensely.

'Well, let me know,' he said, glancing back at Tyler. 'You can't expect too much.'

'Yeah, I know,' said Tyler.

It wasn't clear who they were talking about and I wondered if it was Freya. The conversation shifted to the tides and the possibility of fishing later at the bay further north.

'Do you want me to pass on any messages?'

'No, it's OK,' Tyler replied. He looked distant, although it was hard to read his expression.

Matt paused, a shrewdness in his gaze. He glanced back towards me.

'Freya's with Darcy on the beach,' Tyler said.

I wondered what was happening. It made me think they'd been talking about Freya, that they'd been discussing her when she wasn't here.

I walked out onto the balcony. As I stared down at the rocks below, I noticed someone on the sand as the waves splashed over a platform closer to the cliff. There were a couple of people walking over the rocks around the cliff base, someone running further along on the sand. Perhaps it was Darcy or Freya, I wasn't sure.

I could hear Tyler talking to Matt outside. The tone in their voices sounded more tense now, then Tyler walked back in and began organising a barbecue.

'You seemed quite friendly. I thought there was friction between the two of you.'

'He's OK,' he said, glancing up at me. 'We used to be friends.' He looked at me askance as if I were being sarcastic. 'Anyway, Zac likes him, so I have to keep in good with him. He was just passing through. He's trying to broker a peace between us and Radic. He knows Radic. He had some land near his.'

I studied him suspiciously, sensing he was lying.

He laid out the meat on the barbecue. 'Darcy and Freya had an argument after you left. It was about Kirrily, the little girl who died. I'm worried about Freya's state of mind.' He stepped back from the grill, turning away from me towards the sea. 'Freya doesn't remember it, you know. She thinks Darcy exaggerated something that was an accident, that she wasn't even there when it happened. It wouldn't surprise me.' He moved the meat around with a long prong-shaped fork.

I looked down and could see Freya walking up the driveway, but no Darcy. 'What do you think happened?'

'It was an accident,' he said.

I sat down and watched Tyler turning the meat. It sizzled on the plate, making a spitting sound. Freya walked out onto the balcony. She looked weary and sat down on a seat near the railing. I thought about Tyler's guardedness when he'd been talking with Matt, the unpleasant tone in his voice when he'd said 'Freya's state of mind'.

'Darcy's gone into town. We walked right along the beach. She said she was going to see Julie. I think she'll probably stay there.'

'What about her things?'

'She'll pick them up later.'

Freya slumped back on the seat. I could see she looked troubled as Tyler manoeuvred the meat around. The fork he was using reminded me of the garden tools in the laundry.

Tyler was smiling as he pushed the meat across the metal plate, no doubt happy that Darcy was gone. 'What was it about, Freya, the argument you had when you left?'

'Just some stuff about my father leaving. I haven't seen him for years.'

I thought about my conversation with Darcy the night before, how she wanted Freya to leave Tyler.

Freya went inside and returned with some cutlery. She was dressed in jeans and a light top, a pale pink that flattered her skin and made her look younger. She sat down next to me.

'So you never see your birth father?'

'No. It's not like your own father, Sarah. I haven't seen my stepfather or my birth father for years. I hardly knew my birth father. He left when I was four. He and Darcy barely knew each other when she fell pregnant. I think he only stayed for a while because she was pregnant with me.'

Her arms were pale beneath the top and I could see the light freckling on her skin, similar to Darcy's. She looked away from me and I noticed she'd applied a faint colour in her hair, a subtle tint of red. When I glanced down, I could see an image of a curl on her ankle, like a strange flower.

'But what about what you said about "forgiving"? You said that once, that you have to forgive in order to move on.' I had an ironic tone in my voice, knowing what a cliché it was, that things weren't that simple.

'I'm not that interested, Sarah, not any more.'

'I understand what you mean if it's too toxic.'

'Yes, it is toxic, Sarah. Why would I want to see someone I hardly knew? Tyler never sees his father. He hasn't seen him for years. I was only four when my father left.'

I glanced down at her foot, conscious that there was this avoidance about her birth father again.

'I had it done a while ago,' she said when she saw me looking at the tattoo.

'It looks like an arabesque, or a flower, like the shape I've seen on people's boots around here.'

She moved her foot away. 'The boots are made by a guy from out of town. We all used to hang out in the mountains.' She stretched her foot out, examining the tattoo, turning her ankle around.

I remembered Tyler's carvings back at the house. I wanted to ask them about Scarlett's memorial but decided not to say anything. Instead, I looked across at the house next door as Tyler turned the meat. 'Matt seems well off.'

'Yeah, he is,' said Tyler. 'All the consulting he does, the "worried well" in the city.'

Tyler focused on the meat as Freya picked up a glass, sipping some wine. She held the glass tensely and had a look on her face as if she wished she wasn't there.

I could see Jet through the window. He flicked his head, tail wagging, exploring the house. Glancing up, I noticed a mark on the glass door and remembered the crack in the glass back at Freya and Tyler's. Tyler had cut himself once on a piece of glass at the house in the mountains and there was still a scar there a thick cicatrice, a signature of Tyler's strangeness.

Tyler moved the meat onto a plate and served the steak at the table.

I cut into it, studying the knife. 'Remember that time you cut yourself on the window in the mountains?'

'Yeah, I remember,' he said, sitting down and concentrating on his steak.

I watched him as he reached over and grabbed some bread.

'What happened with your father? What did he say?'

'Very little. He said a guy Liam saw seemed interested in you.'

He studied me now as if this was new information. Freya glanced towards the window. Tyler put his knife and fork down. I had that feeling I'd had when I'd wanted to go down to the beach, to get away from him.

He looked thoughtful and studied me suspiciously. 'You know, I don't blame my mother in a way for having an affair. She just went for the wrong person. I think it was all too much for her in the end, that's why she killed herself.' He looked tight-lipped now.

I watched as he chewed on the steak. Freya wasn't looking at me.

We finished the meal and Tyler began gathering the plates. I walked inside with them and we began stacking the plates from the table into the dishwasher. Tyler had a paranoid look as he went to pick up his glass and knocked it on the floor, swearing.

'Be careful,' Freya called out to him. She went inside to the pantry, handing him the dustpan.

'What are you going to do about Darcy, Freya?'

She picked up the metal fork that Tyler had used for the meat. 'I told you, she's going. If she's trying to undermine us, she shouldn't stay.'

He seemed to relax now and I studied the remnants of meat on the plates. I noticed some fish inside the fridge when Freya opened the door. She seemed to be marinating them and I glanced at the pinkness of the flesh, feeling ill.

'I'm trying not to take it personally,' Tyler said, glancing at me. 'I'm not sure where Darcy's going with all of this.'

I could hear the tension in his voice and wondered what he was referring to. He looked away, and I glanced at the fish, shiny, laid out on the kitchen bench. There was blood coming from the mouth of one where the hook had caught its lips. Freya was turning it over, handling it carefully. I felt sick as Tyler began talking about going out on a cruise to Boral. I caught an unpleasant tone in his voice as I glanced at the fish.

'Can I borrow the car? I want to go into town.'

'Yeah. Where are you going?'

'I just thought I'd look around.'

He seemed unhappy as he reached in his pocket and handed me the car keys. 'We can take Doug's truck but don't be long.'

I walked outside, conscious that he seemed angry. Climbing into the car, I backed it down the driveway. There was someone on the balcony next door as I turned the car and began driving along the road. Water splashed over an outline of rocks down below, a sweep of undulating hills and a darker expanse of trees leading down to the sea. On my right, there was a thicket of trees on a slope leading down to the road.

Approaching the town, I could see rows of buildings, pale blue and brown facades. There was a market near an oval and I parked the car and climbed out, walking towards the stalls. Vegetables were decked out in colourful displays and I continued towards the square, noticing gold-framed paintings, a mirror encircled by designs of scarlet flames. I picked the mirror up, studying my reflection in the glass.

There was a park where children were being escorted on donkey rides. A town crier rang a bell announcing a magician's performance and a short man with pale skin and dark hair appeared on the stage. He was dressed in a jester's costume and stood beside a mysterious box. Children flocked to the stage and he taunted them, asking if any wanted to take their shoes off and walk into the box, but they all backed away.

I smiled at them and noticed an archer in the distance calling a reluctant volunteer up from the audience. A tall gangly man stepped forward and the archer made him sit down in front of a target while a woman held a balloon over his head.

The archer took aim and pulled the bow. The crowd gasped and when I turned I noticed a boy in the crowd. He looked familiar, thin features, pale shaggy blond hair. It was the neighbours' son. He turned away and walked up to another man whose hair was closely shaved in a rounded peak across his scalp to his forehead, a long bristly beard draped across his shirt. He was standing in a defensive position as he watched the archer.

The boy turned and stared back at me. I moved away and approached the stalls. When I turned back, he was still staring at me. He walked back towards the archer. I watched him sauntering slowly, glancing back before he crossed the road. I sensed he was lingering and wanted to approach me, and I remembered how he'd stood on the neighbours' porch, hesitating a moment before moving away. The following day he'd done the same thing, when he was with the horse, standing there watching me. I waited, expecting him to come over, but nothing happened. He stood there with the man, staring back.

I walked back to the car, feeling unsettled. Climbing in and pulling away from the kerb, I began driving along the road and out into the open country. Farmhouses stretched towards the mountain range as I drove deeper into the forest, past tall trees, sunlight streaming between massive trunks.

I reached a turn-off towards the Simpson property where Aden lived. There was a metal gate up ahead and I climbed out to open it before passing through. A man stood in the distance wearing black jeans and a denim jacket. He was talking with a woman dressed in a blue coat, yellow leggings and sandals. Smoke drifted from further away behind the house. A man walked towards the back and as I came closer, I could see that there were more buildings, stretching away towards the bush. The man had a cloud of shaggy dark hair, and as he turned back quickly, I noticed long dreadlocks stretching down to his waist. The sound of bellbirds cut the air, clear and pure, a whipping call that seemed to echo back.

I climbed out of the car and walked towards the man, noticing a woodpile through the mist and an old bath in the yard. He walked back towards me and I studied his thin lips and angular jawline.

'Is Aden here?

He nodded in the direction of the bush. 'Up the back.'

There was another house further along and a shed in front, a cabin further out towards the bush. It seemed to be some kind of commune and I remembered the garage and shed at the back of Freya and Tyler's place near the bush, the strange collection of objects and bedclothes on the floor, the imprint that looked too large for a dog. There was a paddock between the house and shed. The man with dreadlocks was in the distance, walking away from me. He continued towards the bush.

To my right, I noticed three horses roaming in a field, a chestnut, a black and a piebald. They were chasing each other, with a sense of urgency as if they were fleeing from something, the wind or an unseen force. I remembered the wooden horse back at Freya's place, the one that Alison had given her, the one she'd broken as a child.

Further along, there were two large metal buildings, corrugated-iron sheds, with tree ferns around them. A sharp sound of metal hitting metal rent the air, the cackling of hens and roosters scrubbing in the dirt. The metallic sound was coming from the shed. Liam had said he'd done some metal work with a man who lived in the bush.

I approached the door and saw a man hitting metal with a hammer, sparks flying. He was older, with full lips, pale skin, heavy arms. I stood there, watching the metal soften in the fire, then cool down in oil. He hit the object on an anvil. There was a collection of knives and axes lined up, and the ornate handles reminded me of the vase made by Zac. The man had a shaved head, and sturdy build.

There was a lull in the noise and he must have realised I was standing there, as he looked up. His expression softened a little into a slightly distant smile. He put the metal down.

'I'm looking for Aden.'

He studied me for a moment. 'Aden's up at the house.'

He returned to the metal, not wanting to talk, and I moved away, thinking about the knife my father had carried and the time he'd killed our dog.

I walked towards the house. It had two storeys, with verandas at each level, the eaves supported by columns resembling fluted or twisted poles. A dog with tan fur was sitting on a worn mat, near the corner of the veranda. It looked like the dog I'd seen in the forest when I was walking with Jet and it glanced up at me with soft doe eyes. Odd that it was so different to Jet, who always seemed agitated and whose eyes often had a menacing look. I glanced at the dog. It raised its head slightly as I knocked.

After a few moments, the door opened and a woman stood before me. She had dark hair, long to her shoulders, and a black dress that came down to around her calves, black flat-soled shoes. There was an aroma of roasting coffee drifting down the hallway.

The woman stared back at me for a moment. She was tall, pretty and had similar dark eyes to myself, a similar way of dressing. 'You're Sarah, aren't you? You look so much like your brother.' She led me into a sitting room.

In the light, the wall had a dark purplish hue with blotches of light and colour. I glanced to my right at tables on either side with lamps. Her face was thin, oval-shaped, framed by dark hair. She stared not at me but into the distance. The windows had a patterned cream and black design, the slats of the blind screening off the outside world and light. I sat down and shifted my position on the couch.

'I'm Gisela, Billy's girlfriend.'

She was probably looking for a resemblance to my father but there wasn't any. Liam and I mostly looked like our mother. I watched her lean back on the couch.

A man walked into the room. He looked familiar and I recognised him as Aden Lonegan, the man I'd seen at the pub.

'Aden, this is Sarah, Liam's sister.'

Aden was tall, dark eyes, broad cheekbones and a ruddy complexion. The tan dog walked in and Gisela turned towards it. Aden seemed to be weighing something up as if he were assessing whether to trust me. I sensed he was about to tell me something.

'Celeste told me she saw you.'

There was silence as I watched Gisela patting the dog. A dragonfly mobile was hanging from a light in the corridor, spinning back and forth and then twisting in a frenzy.

I was conscious of someone behind me, coming from an adjoining room, and when I turned a man walked in. He sat down on a cane chair in the corner. His head was bowed and when he looked up, I recognised him immediately as the man in the forest. His skin was swarthy, eyes an intense black, heavy eyebrows and hollow cheekbones. I could see that glint of intelligence and noticed that his chin was covered by stubble. He seemed older than I remembered, and the attractiveness of his face was marred by the heavy dent or scar down the side. He picked up a knife from the table and twisted something out of his shoe, a piece of twig. I studied the strange dent again, thinking that it looked like a scar. Yes, it was a scar, perhaps from a knife, an incident that might have happened in a fight.

I glanced across the room and remembered standing at the gaping hole in the floor at Liam's house, staring down into the blackness of the earth beneath, and then back at the mottled patterns on the wall and the ash on the floor.

'Sarah, this is Niall.'

So this was Tyler's mother's lover. Freya had said his name was Niall Price. He stared back at me, his eyes, that intense black, heavy lashes. I remembered Tyler's relationship with his father. Niall was wearing a dark shirt, blue jeans and boots. I saw his hat on a chair nearby, the one he'd worn in the forest. His boots were plain with no curl insignia like the boots I'd seen worn by the other men around here, or the design on Freya's ankle. The hat was similar to the one I'd seen worn by Radic's brother.

He went back to twisting the twig from his shoe as if he were contemplating what to say. Gisela was sitting opposite in an old arm chair. The black dress she was wearing covered her knees and flowed down along her legs. She had an exotic look that complemented her clothes, black tights and shoes.

Niall leant forward. 'How are they? Your friends. I suppose you know about Tyler's mother. He had a hand in it all.' He had that sarcastic tone in his voice, the same tone he'd had in the forest.

I glanced around the room, feeling nervous. There were dark windows, a wooden chest, and a green arm-roll sofa. I noticed a clock and studied the numbers as they moved forward, a sense that time was ticking slowly, everything was suspended but also moving forward, and I willed myself to focus. 'We're at Doug's at the moment,' I said.

Niall had a look now which was difficult to read. Through the window I could see one of the horses. It had strayed towards the house. When I turned, Niall's expression had shifted. He stood up and walked to the window. The horse swished its tail. It was standing by the window, the pale sheen of its flank contrasting with the dark of Niall's hair. It raised its neck and whinnied before coming closer.

I remembered the wooden statue of the horse back at Freya's, how she'd kept it and I wondered if it symbolised freedom for her. I wondered how well Liam knew them all, what he'd been doing out here.

Niall turned back and stared at me with a surly look. The tan dog was shuffling around near the couch. It seemed so placid and different to Jet. Niall pushed the dog away with his foot. His long legs were stretched out across the floor as he sat down, dominating the corner of the room. I glanced at his boots again and studied his dark curly hair, dusky skin, high cheekbones and thin lips.

I didn't know what to say as I eyed the dog cautiously and I began thinking about Tyler and the fighting cocks in Indonesia. Tyler had been angry about it. He thought it was terrible, deliberately abusing animals for their aggression, dogs fighting too. It seemed strange that he would be angry about aggression towards dogs and yet harm a human being. People can be like that, though, kind towards animals and then have an intense antipathy towards humans and particular people. There was Zac's treatise on the Internet too about the person who had changed their life and I wondered if it was Tyler.

Niall picked up a pale-coloured biscuit from the floor and held his hand out to the dog. The dog walked up and took the biscuit from him, chomping into it.

'Of course Tyler wasn't happy about my relationship with his mother. He was completely influenced by his father.'

Gisela looked away. Her small heart-shaped face, dark eyes, long thick wavy hair, reminded me of my mother. Her head was tilted back slightly giving her an almost remote look, a bit like a pared-down version of my mother.

I studied the way Niall was watching her intently. 'You might be focusing too much on Tyler,' I said.

Niall looked at me coldly. 'I don't think so. You should talk to Freya about it. She knows what happened.'

Gisela wrapped her arms around herself as if trying to keep warm. I glanced up at the dark recesses of the room, the cobwebby corner. I thought I saw a centipede squirm across the floor but it was just a dark piece of thread. That feeling of distrust returned.

'Talk to her if you want. See if she'll admit anything.'

Niall looked at me ironically and I felt anxious, a feeling that I'd been duped.

'Come back and tell me what she says.'

'How well do you know them?'

'I knew Tyler when he was young and I know Freya's stepfather. He thinks Tyler told her what happened with Grace, his mother. His father killed her and Tyler helped or the other way around.'

'I will talk to her,' I said.

I stared back at him angrily as he began talking about Tyler's father, how Tyler was completely under his sway, how he'd interfered in Grace's life and how neither of them understood her. I listened patiently but he seemed to be raving. There was something unbalanced about him.

'What goes around comes around,' he said.

I decided I'd better go. I didn't trust them and stood up, wondering if they'd follow me as I told them I needed to see Freya and walked outside.

When I reached the car, I glanced back at the buildings, the way they disappeared towards the bush, the shed where the man was working on the knives. Climbing in, I began driving back through the mountains and along the coast, wondering if these were the people Connor had seen the day before. I tried ringing him but there was no answer.

After I'd been driving for some time, a ridge appeared and Doug's house came into view. I parked the car at the top of the driveway and gazed up at the house next door, windows opaque and distant. There was no one on the balcony as I walked to the door. I noticed someone bending down through the doorway. It was Freya. She had a sullen expression as she walked into the room. Jet was beside her. She sat down and I stared at her, feeling distrustful.

'I just saw Niall Price out at the Simpson property. He thinks Tyler was involved in his mother's death. They seemed to think you know more about it.'

Jet was at her feet and she glanced down at him.

'There was a man out at Radic's once but I didn't know who he was. They didn't introduce him. I knew they'd do something like this. He probably wants to extort money out of Tyler or his father.' She sounded anxious and was looking away from me. 'People think Tyler's father had influence but he didn't. There's no evidence at all that it was anything other than suicide.' She turned back now, studying me impassively from the couch.

I gazed back at her and she looked at me uncomfortably.

'Anyway, Niall's disturbed. Julie told me. We talked about it a while ago. I asked her about it. She spoke to Radic. It's because they all have axes to grind.'

She leant back on the couch away from Jet. She gazed back at me and I noticed her expression shift slightly.

'How do you know he's disturbed?'

She sighed and turned away from me. 'It's just what I've heard from Julie.'

I could see her in profile as she turned towards the window, the straight slightly tilted nose, delicate chin, her strong arms beneath the pink top she was wearing. I had a sense that she'd put up an emotional fortress. There was something uncertain about her. She stood up and walked out to the balcony, leaning against the railing as she studied the ocean below. I followed her, thinking it was true, Niall had seemed disturbed.

'Someone told me she was depressed, you know, the type to commit suicide. It does play on your mind, all the suspicions. But when I looked into it, it was all exaggerated. I don't think it's true, Sarah. There hasn't been any evidence, that's why I've been thinking of getting away from here. I'm sick of it all. The way they target people. You got away from it and now you've been drawn back into it. I'm sorry that's happened, Sarah.'

That image of her concentrating on her knitting came into my mind, head bowed, completely focused as she wound the wool around the needles, clacking them back and forth.

She leant over the balcony, looking down, contemplating the rocks and waves. 'That's how it is. They scapegoat people. Niall's probably had a general grievance against Tyler for some time.'

'Maybe you should go to the police.'

She walked out the back and I followed her, thinking that she reminded me a little of Darcy, something cunning in her. A bird flew down to the water in an old birdbath in the yard, splashing as it tried to land, dipping its claws and then flapping backwards, drops of water glinting in the sunlight. There was a bench and some gardening tools nearby. I thought about Tyler's expression when he was talking about his mother. He'd seemed guarded, angry, but then he seemed to have come to terms with it. There were pot plants and weeds, a knife near a pot of ferns. I bent down and picked up the knife, studying it. I began slicing the stems of weeds, my hands moving mechanically with the rhythm of my thoughts, the knife flicking back and forth between the leaves.

A cat was curled up in the shade of a hibiscus plant and through the broken paling in the fence, I could see Jet in the corner. He gazed up at me and I remembered the painting of the two girls back at Ivy's place, the flower dominating the landing in a menacing way. The house was silent now and Freya had left the yard. I stood up and walked to the doorway.

Freya was somewhere in the house and when I found her, she looked at me uncertainly. There was a slight look of anxiety in her eyes and I remembered the figures further along the beach. They'd run towards the water and dipped below the waves, swimming back towards the shore, pulling themselves up and walking towards the sand.

'Zac used to light fires,' she said. 'It was before we knew you, Sarah.'

'Do you think he lit the fire that killed Liam?'

'I don't know, but I think he's been involved with the Lonegans.'

She stood up and I followed her outside. I could see a dark silhouette in the bush as she walked away from me towards the edge.

'What's the matter?'

'Nothing. I don't know if Lola's still alive, if Zac knows where she is. There's something strange about it.'

For some reason, I thought of that journey on Doug's boat. I tried not to think about the fish dying on the floor of the boat, how I hadn't wanted to eat once-living creatures that I'd just seen die a horrible death. Trying to calm down, I told myself that this was ridiculous but I began thinking about cruising out into the deep water on Doug's boat.

Freya began walking through the trees, deeper into the bush. I followed her.

She called back to me as I caught up. 'There's something not right.'

She was a little ahead of me now and I saw her bending down near a tree as if she were hunting for something. She pulled ahead again, looking unhappy, and I tried to catch up with her. She seemed angry, I could see it in her face, and I walked with her through the bush but she kept pulling ahead. I sensed she was trying to get somewhere urgently. When I pulled up level with her, she looked disheartened and seemed to be staring down into a gully.

I noticed the black silhouettes of trees in the distance, a greyness, and the brilliant white circle of the moon, the darkness of the trees, branches hanging low.

'The last anyone heard of Lola, she was out here.' Freya paused for a moment, staring down below. She seemed to be focusing on the gully and had that pensive look on her face. 'I've been thinking about things, about Liam's death,' she said. 'I think it was an accident. Not a suicide but maybe a suicidal wish that led him to not be careful.'

Anguished, I looked at her. I could tell she was trying to say that he mightn't have actively killed himself but had lost the will to live.

'I think he tried to help Lola. He wanted her to get out of it all, away from the Lonegans and her family.'

She stared out into the bush then began climbing down. 'It's been bothering me for a while, the whole thing.'

She looked down below and I noticed a mound of earth as I walked down towards the stream, slipping and sliding so that my jeans became muddy. I was concentrating on the slope until I reached the bottom. I glanced around quickly but there was no one there, only a profusion of leaves and tree trunks. I sensed something behind me, conscious again of an unpleasant feeling, someone watching, further back beyond the trees. There were pieces of wood on the ground, a camp, and I stood up quickly. I began walking swiftly, and I thought I saw someone through the trees walking towards me, a white dog, its jaw slack so that I could see the sharp outline of its teeth.

When I turned, Freya was nowhere to be seen. The dog reared

up growling, its teeth white against the dirty shade of its fur. I saw a man moving through the bush, the broad brim of his hat dark against the pale shape of his face. He was walking towards a woman in the distance, tall and slim like Freya, then he turned back, walking towards me like a tracker in the dying shadows of the sun.